The Scou  *...er*

The Scoundrel's Wager

Laura A. Barnes

Laura A. Barnes

2020

First Printing: 2020

ISBN: 9798638838201

Laura A. Barnes

Website: **www.lauraabarnes.com**

Cover Art by Cheeky Covers

Editor: Polgarus Studios

To William:

My very own scoundrel.

Happy 30th Wedding Anniversary!

Chapter One

"Kathleen, please attend Lady Holdenburg in the parlor. I must gather my notes," Lady Beckwith asked Kathleen, breezing past her daughter's bedroom.

"Yes, Mama."

Kathleen brushed out her skirts after she rose from her chair. She slid the deck of cards into a desk drawer before she left and hurried to the parlor, excited to visit with the Duchess of Norbrooke. Her mother's friend shared a love of the theater, and Kathleen wanted to discuss the newest play to hit London. Also, it wouldn't hurt to have another woman's opinion on which color of dress she should wear to the Camville Ball tomorrow evening. Kathleen found the duchess to be a likable character—unlike her son. How such an enlightened woman had an annoying son such as Devon Holdenburg was beyond her. There wasn't a gentleman more frustrating.

"Your Grace, what a delight." Kathleen entered the parlor. Her steps came to a halt once she encountered the lady's son instead. Kathleen glanced around to discover she was alone with the earl.

"And is it a delight to welcome me too?" Holdenburg asked.

"My mother informed me that the duchess would be in the parlor."

"She was. However, Dallis tempted her away with a view of the nursery."

"I will join them."

"And leave me all alone?"

"It would not be proper to be alone with you," Kathleen replied, turning to leave.

"There is nobody present to take notice. In addition, our families are longtime friends. Nothing would be untoward."

"You are forgetting one thing, my lord."

"What might that be, my lady?"

"That I do not wish to be alone with you. I endure your company when I have to in the presence of others. Other than that, I find you barely tolerable."

"What have I done to bring about this warm regard?" Lord Holdenburg asked with humor lighting his eyes.

"You have shown me nothing but indifference in the past. Why, now, the sudden change? Have you ruined the latest round of debutantes?"

"You are aware, my dear, that I do not ruin any debutante that does not wish to be ruined. I have heard no complaints thus far. Have you? If so, please tell, so I may alter my seductions."

"Why, you insufferable brute."

Holdenburg shouldn't try to raise her ire. But he found Kathleen so entertaining when her temper rose. He'd meant to accompany his mother to the Beckwiths' with the intention of courting Kathleen. He decided now was the time, since Lady Beckwith had Rory settled with Dallis, and Devon was no longer needed. He wanted Kathleen as his. Holdenburg observed the love shared between Rory and Dallis and wanted the same thing for himself. And the only lady for him was Kathleen. He had patiently waited for her to bloom into the lady she had become. When Kathleen started to slander

Devon, it set him to prod her temper. Since Devon began this behavior, he might as well continue and start the courting another day. Unless he **could** turn the situation around somehow.

Kathleen fumed at Holdenburg. She tried to call him out on his ungentlemanly behavior and he turned it around into his pleasure. The nerve of the man to think she would give him pointers to ruin her friends. Even though every single one of them wished for a private moment in Holdenburg's company. She'd watched many of them try, and a few succeeded. He would dance and steal away with them into dark gardens. Then after a short time had passed, the lady would sneak back into the ballroom, a blush gracing her cheeks and a satisfied smile. Shortly thereafter, Holdenburg always swaggered back in with his usual conceited expression. Each of their smiles confirmed of a secret rendezvous that appeased both parties. Kathleen would sit and listen to the tittering of the lady gushing over the seductive skills of Devon Holdenburg. Kathleen silently fumed when other ladies applauded his attributes. There could be no other reason than a lack of respect that explained why she found his actions scandalous. None at all. Now he sat here proud of himself. The insufferable boor.

"If you will excuse me, my lord. I wish to seek your mother's opinion on which dress I should wear tomorrow evening." Kathleen started for the door.

"Of course, Lady Kathleen, time spent in your company has been charming as always." Holdenburg bowed. "If you want my opinion, I prefer you in blue, a dark sapphire."

"I wasn't aware I asked your opinion, my lord."

"Nonetheless, I offered it."

Before Kathleen replied, her mother returned to the parlor. She was carrying an envelope.

"Here you are, my lord. You will find I applied great detail on your requests. I hope you find them advantageous enough to meet your needs."

Holdenburg slid the envelope inside the pocket of his suit coat. Lady Beckwith had agreed to help him with his plan of attack against her daughter. The very daughter who held no clue of Holdenburg's feelings for her. Whenever they were in the same company, Kathleen brought out the devil in him. Her hatred kept him fueled to antagonize her. The very opposite of true desire. But the circumstances of their relationship always caused this war of words.

"What requests?" Kathleen asked.

"Nothing, my dear. A private matter between the earl and myself. Where has your mother gotten to?" she asked Devon.

"Dallis is giving her a tour of the nursery."

Kathleen said, "I wanted the duchess's opinion on which color of dress to wear for tomorrow evening."

Devon said, "I told her she would look lovely in a deep sapphire gown."

"Lord Holdenburg, you know Kathleen must wear pastels."

"A pity."

"Which dresses do you wish her to choose from?" Lady Beckwith asked.

"Either the pale pink or the soft blue we bought last week," replied Kathleen.

"Since Lord Holdenburg would like to see you in blue, why don't you wear the blue tomorrow evening?" said Lady Beckwith.

"The pink it is," Kathleen countered, leaving the parlor.

Kathleen refused to stay in the same room with his smug lordship one moment longer. Why her mother always tried to please Holdenburg confused her. It was if her mother knew something she didn't. Blue. Humph. While the pink wasn't her favorite choice, she would wear it. Anything to go against him.

Lady Beckwith watched Kathleen, in a snit, leave the parlor. She waited patiently for her daughter to acknowledge Lord Holdenburg as the catch he was, and Kathleen stubbornly refused. When she viewed the amused expression on his face, Lady Beckwith realized Holdenburg took great pleasure in Kathleen's aggravation.

"I don't even know if my suggestions will help you."

"Any insight will be of great assistance," he said.

"Will we see you tomorrow evening?"

"I wouldn't miss seeing Lady Kathleen in her pink confection twirling across the ballroom floor."

"And will you offer for a dance?"

"She will only refuse."

"How do you know, unless you ask?"

"Perhaps tomorrow I will."

Devon went in search for his mother, with Lady Beckwith following. If they didn't leave soon, the ladies would be late for their charitable meeting. They found her in the foyer and in a lively discussion with Kathleen about a new play he had invited the Beckwiths' to attend with his family next week. Thankfully, Kathleen's aggravation towards him did not extend towards his mother. While he would love to have her warm regards directed towards him, Devon quite enjoyed their sparring matches.

Lady Beckwith said, "Kathleen, we are running behind for our meeting. Do you wish to accompany us? Dallis is coming along."

"No, Mama. I have some correspondence I must attend to."

Devon said, "That is too bad. I had hoped to convince you to take a walk in the park while I wait for the lovely ladies to attend their meeting."

"What an excellent idea, Devon," said the duchess.

Holdenburg's request placed Kathleen in a delicate spot. She couldn't deny him while his mother approved of the outing. If she were to refuse, it would make her less favorable in the duchess's eyes, and her mother would later lecture Kathleen on her manners. She felt her mother's eyes on her, sending a silent message. Kathleen pasted a smile on her face before she replied.

"That sounds like a delightful idea, my lord."

Holdenburg smiled smugly, knowing he'd succeeded. Well, he might have won this hand, but Kathleen would make their outing difficult. Their walk would not be a long one.

"Excellent, shall we ladies?" Holdenburg held out his hands to usher them to his carriage.

The two older ladies gathered on each side of Dallis, linking their arms together, discussing the meeting they were about to attend. Which left Kathleen to walk alongside Holdenburg. The earl took a liberty that shouldn't be allowed by placing his hand on the small of her back, walking them toward the carriage. His touch sent warm shivers tickling throughout her body. The intimate act brought forth kinder thoughts towards him. She shouldn't allow him, but couldn't call him out in front of their mothers. She would wait until they were alone to address his inappropriate behavior. Kathleen must keep her temper around him or else Holdenburg would push past her wall of anger. She had an agenda for the remainder of the season and becoming soft around Lord Devon Holdenburg wasn't part of her plan.

Devon knew he pushed the boundaries by touching Kathleen so intimately, but he couldn't resist. The temptation of her closeness and the company of others urged him toward his improper act. Devon knew that once he delivered the other ladies at the Hartridges' then he would have to face her wrath at his improprieties. He waited with anticipation. Kathleen would fill his ears with a fiery tirade. The first on her list would be cornering her into an outing after she couldn't say nay without disappointing their mothers.

He felt Kathleen stiffen, but she didn't pull away. To do so would draw attention toward them. His fingers stroked across where her back curved into her buttocks. How he wished he could caress lower. Much lower. Where there were no garments restricting him from the silkiness of her skin. Would the rest of her body blush as her cheeks did so now? Soon. He would learn the answers to his questions. Soon. Lady Kathleen Beckwith was unaware of the game he played. However, by the end of the season, she would be in his arms, moaning his name.

Chapter Two

After arriving at the Hartridge townhome, Devon and Kathleen started off for the private park. Devon's footman followed at a discreet distance, acting as a chaperone. Their walk took them inside the park and a bench near the water. Behind his back, Devon gave his footman a signal to leave them alone once he noticed the park was empty. If Kathleen meant to give him a set down, then he didn't need a servant observing to gossip about it later. When Kathleen stayed silent after quite a while, Devon decided to prompt her.

"Unleash your fury, my lady. 'Tis only you and I to hear the passionate lecture you wish to give."

Kathleen turned to pierce Holdenburg with a glare that would shake terror in any other man. However, Holdenburg sat amused. Damn him.

"You are not worth the anger you attempt to provoke me into. I am only enduring this outing to pacify our mothers. Why you have asked for my company is beyond me. And I, for one, do not care. Now, if you do not mind, I wish to enjoy the beauty of the day. After what I deem to be a measurable amount of time, I will return to the Hartridges' where I shall pretend to take an interest in their charitable meeting. When I am questioned, I will be the lady my mother has raised me to be and praise your gentlemanly attentions."

There were only two ways Devon could react. One would be to act the gentleman his mother raised him to be and sit there silently. Or the other alternative would be to antagonize Kathleen into the kind of reaction which fired his blood. The first option would work better for his plans to court her properly. The other held more of a temptation. There was nothing he enjoyed more than provoking Kathleen Beckwith. It would appear that the devilish side of himself would win today. Devon might as well finish strong, since he started this role earlier at the Beckwith's residence. Tomorrow he would start anew. Today, he needed this for whatever reason there may be.

"I asked you on this walk, my dear, to enjoy your company. I feel we have gotten off to the wrong start this season. It is my greatest hope to rectify our situation. However, since you hold only displeasure at my company, I must give you more of a reason for your distaste." Devon brushed a tendril of hair loose from the knot behind her ear, his finger trailing down her neck. "I also have ulterior motives for my reason, for requesting time alone with you."

Kathleen stilled at his touch. Just as from before, a shiver tingled along her neck at his caress. She didn't understand why this unsettled her.

"And that would be?" Kathleen whispered.

Devon saw her stillness and knew he rattled her. Good. He slid closer on the bench and lowered his head to brush his lips across where his fingers had trailed. Devon inhaled her sweetness and let it sink into his soul. The scent of lilies enflamed his senses. He couldn't resist the temptation. Devon ached for Kathleen. Throughout the season he had wanted this. Even when he'd courted Lady Dallis MacPherson, he had only wanted this. Only ever this. He'd waited patiently for Kathleen to bloom, and now that she had, Devon would pluck the womanhood from her.

Devon's lips continued a path to her mouth. When Kathleen didn't push him away and instead sighed, he didn't stop. Devon only wanted a small sample to appease him until tomorrow. Then he would be the proper gentleman and not the scoundrel she believed him to be.

Soft and slow, his tongue traced her lips. When she opened them, he took what he could no longer deny himself. He took possession of her lips, stroking his need. Devon pulled Kathleen in his arms and devoured her. The sensation of her on his tongue opened up to a treasure of forbidden treats. Each drag of his mouth across hers tempted him. When Kathleen opened under him, he was lost. Her tongue joined his, stroking their desires. Devon tightened his hold, pushing her breasts against his chest. To treat himself to those sweet things would be his greatest pleasure. Devon forgot their whereabouts when he slid his hand inside her dress. His fingers stroked across her nipple and he captured her gasp when he pinched the bud into a tight ball of need.

Kathleen was lost. Lost in the arms of the scoundrel, Lord Holdenburg. His touch and kiss tempted her into a wild scandal. Was this how every debutante felt when he ruined them in the gardens? At least he gave the other ladies privacy. With her, he seduced her in the open where anybody could walk upon them. Kathleen's mind tried to resist and call a halt to Devon's actions, but her body held a different opinion. Her body screamed for him to take her. When the cool breeze caressed her breasts, Kathleen's mind returned from its fog and pushed Devon away. What more liberties had she allowed him?

Devon dropped his arms when she pushed at him. Both of them breathed heavily while they tried to calm their emotions. Kathleen straightened her dress and looked everywhere but at him. The blush sweeping across her cheeks continued along her neck to her ... His gaze followed where the blush headed, the same place he wished to devour. Damn. What had he done? He glanced around the park to see if they were still alone. When the park proved empty except for them, he breathed a sigh of relief. Not that he wouldn't have made their situation right. The end result would be what he planned, but Devon wanted their courtship to play out in a different way. If he meant to court Kathleen properly, then Devon must make sure they were never left alone.

His gaze brushed across Kathleen again, and he realized he should apologize. But to apologize would mean he regretted what transpired between them. And he didn't regret one single, delectable second. Heaven. Pure heaven. That was how Kathleen felt when he kissed her. Devon reacted the only way he could. He rose and offered Kathleen his arm. He didn't want to provoke her anger any more or have either of them saying something they would regret.

Kathleen looked at his offered arm and wanted to refuse it. Didn't she? Yes, she did. Her emotions felt like they were scattered about the park. She wanted to reprimand him for the scoundrel he was, but couldn't. Kathleen enjoyed his kiss too much for the call out. Her body wouldn't let her betray her mind. She slid an arm into his and allowed Devon to guide her to the Hartridge's. He never once attempted to apologize or strike up a conversation.

Inside, Kathleen quietly slipped in next to her mother, trying not to bring attention upon herself. Which was an easy task, because Holdenburg drew all the ladies' attention his way. He charmed everyone in the room, doting on each of them with a compliment to blush. Each lady was married, but that didn't stop them from eagerly soaking up the earl's words. Kathleen rolled her eyes at their gullibility. When her gaze encountered Devon's, the heat coming from them froze Kathleen in her seat. As he kept up his litany of compliments, Devon never broke his gaze and she never looked away. Kathleen didn't understand how to handle the emotions he stirred. She broke Devon's gaze, wiping her palms on her dress, trying to join the conversation with her mother and the Duchess of Norbrooke. But talking to Devon's mother only increased her uneasiness. How did one hold a perfectly normal conversation with the mother of a scoundrel who'd just kissed her passionately in the park? She couldn't, not without blurting out her son's indiscretion. Then that would only set a drama Kathleen didn't wish for. Instead, Kathleen excused herself with a promise to visit the duchess next week for their discussion on the new play.

Kathleen joined a smaller group of younger ladies in the corner. Dallis chatted with Lady Sidney Wildeburg and Lady Sophia Langley, the Duchess of Sheffield. The two ladies had been friends of Rory's for years and had welcomed Dallis into their tight circle. While Kathleen held their acquaintance, she was a few years younger and ran with a different circle. But still, at every occasion, they extended their friendship to Kathleen.

"Did you enjoy your walk with Lord Holdenburg?" Dallis asked.

A blush immediately warmed Kathleen's face. She needed to convince these ladies that the walk had been innocent. It didn't help Kathleen that Holdenburg's gaze still rested on her. Why did he stare at her so intimately amongst these women? Devon made his intentions more than obvious.

Kathleen kept the description of their outing simple. "We shared a pleasant walk through the park."

"It must have been very pleasant, if your blush has anything to say," Sidney said.

"Tis not a blush, but a result of the warm weather. I became a trifle overheated, and Lord Holdenburg saw to my comfort by escorting me out of the heat."

"Mmm, so you say, my dear," Sidney replied.

"I know if I spent any time alone with Lord Holdenburg, I would blush too," Sophia teased.

"For shame, Phee. You are a married lady. Your Grace, Alex, is pleasing to the eye."

"For shame on you, Dallis. You are a married lady too. Too newly wed to be admiring my Alex."

"Then I must be very shameful, because I find all of our husbands quite appealing. However, the lord we are discussing has a dark aura surrounding him that heightens the imagination," said Sidney.

The ladies laughed, teasing each other. Once again, a conversation Kathleen needed to extract herself from. Especially when her brother, Rory, was one of the gentlemen they discussed. Luckily, the appearance of Rory and Lord Hartridge saved Kathleen from their silly discussion. Since their meeting had ended, Rory and Lord Hartridge joined the ladies for tea, which turned into socializing. Kathleen left her friends and sat next to Lord Hartridge, asking him questions on his latest research project. A safe subject that would keep her thoughts from becoming occupied by Devon Holdenburg. Also, talking with Lord Hartridge wouldn't bring about any questions she didn't wish to answer.

Since Rory was already at the Hartridges, he would escort them home. They wouldn't have to rely on Holdenburg's generosity. Kathleen informed Rory that she would wait for them in the carriage. She needed to leave before Holdenburg cornered her into another conversation where she couldn't refuse him without everybody noticing.

Holdenburg saw Kathleen slip from the room. While every inch of him wanted to follow, nay needed to follow, he resisted. There would be plenty of time later. There were too many watchful eyes present. Any interactions he had with Kathleen, he wanted to keep to himself. Even though, in those moments, Kathleen spent them denying her feelings toward him. Holdenburg knew he played a dangerous game with the way his eyes pursued Kathleen while she chatted with the other ladies. He couldn't help himself. She was too irresistible. Holdenburg noticed Kathleen's discomfort while talking to his mother and chuckled to himself. When she joined her friends in the corner, her blush darkened. He wondered why, and figured it must have had something to do with their walk. Their teasing led Kathleen to join Lord Hartridge in a discussion. Once she took notice of the other guest's departures, she snuck away. Since Rory was here, he would escort his family home. Holdenburg gathered his mother, and they spoke their goodbyes.

Before they left, Devon's mother stopped to congratulate Beckwith on the announcement of his impending child. His parents had been away for most of the season at their family's estate. They preferred the life in the country than to London's busy season. But a few key discussions in Parliament brought them back to the city.

"Holdenburg."

"Beckwith."

Each man acknowledged the other with a stilted nod, not wanting to incur their mothers' wrath. Devon's mother was unaware that they were no longer old chums and the reason behind it. Lady Beckwith knew of the circumstances and encouraged Holdenburg to show patience. That, in time, Rory would accept the reasons for his father's demise and realize Devon's actions were meant to prevent the awful outcome. While Devon missed his close friendship with Rory, it wasn't a priority. There was only one person he wanted to please, and after today it would be more difficult than ever to achieve that goal.

"How was your walk with Kathleen?" his mother inquired as they walked toward their carriage.

Devon noticed that Rory heard the question when he turned to glare. He sighed at Rory's glare. Rory made it perfectly clear a few years ago that Devon was never to be alone with Kathleen. Rory would tolerate his presence in the company of their mothers, but other than that Devon was never to step foot near Kathleen. Devon understood Rory's protection of his sister. But it was for the wrong reasons. Devon had injected himself into that fateful card game and raised the stakes for the very same reason. He only wanted to protect Kathleen, never to harm her. However, the bloke was too rash to see otherwise.

"Quite enjoyable, mother," answered Devon.

"Kathleen is a dear girl. She would be a great catch, my dear."

"Holdenburg," Rory growled from behind.

"Yes, mother, you are correct, she would be."

Devon baited Rory. He knew Rory wouldn't call him out in front of his mother. Even though his tone said it all, he needed to make it clear to Rory that he wouldn't be cowed by the man. Devon stayed away all these years not because of Rory's threats, but for Kathleen to enjoy what all young debutantes enjoy: shopping, soirees, luncheons, being paid court too. Before he staked his claim. Now Devon planned to court Kathleen, and Rory wouldn't be a hinderance to his plans.

He stopped and turned his mother and himself around to face Rory.

"Yes, Beckwith?"

Rory scowled. "A word, please."

The Duchess of Norbrooke said, "Rory, dear, what a delight Dallis is. You are a lucky man. A treasure to behold. A shame my Devon could not capture her for himself."

"Thank you, Duchess. Your compliments mean the world to me."

Rory decided this wasn't the place for his confrontation with Holdenburg. No, he would clear this matter later. It would appear he needed to reinforce his threat about staying away from Kathleen. Rory had watched Holdenburg's attentions toward Dallis a few months ago and knew the reprobate to be a danger to his sister's reputation. He wouldn't have Kathleen ruined by this scoundrel. Rory tightened his fists behind his back to hide his anger.

"Never mind. Perhaps I will see you at the club later. I have an issue with a bill I would like your support with."

Holdenburg's twisted smile displayed that he knew Rory's excuse to talk was pure rubbish.

"Perhaps," was all that Holdenburg would grant Beckwith.

Chapter Three

"Did you see the blush gracing her cheeks?" asked Sophia.

"Or the scorching gaze he sent her way?" said Sidney, fanning herself.

"The heat consumed the room. Oh, the poor dear, she has gained Holdenburg's full assault," replied Dallis.

"Was he overpowering when he courted you?" asked Sophia.

"He tried. But I was too far gone in love with Rory to take notice."

"Oh, my. Now, my Wilde, he has enough charm to keep me content. But the smoldering coming off in waves from Holdenburg can make a lady reconsider," said Sidney.

Dallis said, "I should keep this knowledge to myself, but I wish for them to find the same happiness we have found in our marriages. While we were courting, Holdenburg admitted to his feelings for Kathleen. And I noticed Kathleen was not indifferent to him. I do not think she is aware of what her feelings are, but I think she shares the same affections as him. I know Holdenburg holds a secret that could very well be his demise."

"Perhaps, my services would be of some use?" said Sidney.

"Your services?"

"Sidney fashions herself a matchmaker," said Sophia.

"I do not fashion. I am. Are Sheffield and you not married? Did Dallis and Rory not find their happily ever after?"

"As always, you are correct Sidney," Sophia agreed.

"What is Sidney correct on?" asked Rory, coming up from behind to rest a hand on Dallis's shoulder.

"On my matchmaking abilities."

Rory groaned. "Not again. Who are the unlucky participants this time?"

"Why your very own—"

"Oh." Dallis shook her head to her friends and lifted a hand to her mouth, turning with wide eyes to Rory.

"What is it, my dear?"

"I feel nauseous all of a sudden."

"You have overdone it this afternoon. If you would please excuse us, ladies, I must get my wife home to rest."

Rory, not taking any cautions with Dallis, lifted her in his arms to carry her to the carriage. He knew he overdid it, but Dallis's health was his main priority. He would need to put a halt to her activities. Rory thought the morning sickness had passed, but it would appear Dallis still suffered from this pregnancy affliction.

Dallis wanted to roll her eyes at Rory's overprotective measures— having faked her illness. But she couldn't have Sidney telling Rory their plans to play matchmaker between Kathleen and Holdenburg. Rory only tolerated the man due to their mothers' friendship. He wouldn't want any interactions between his sister and his once-trusted friend, now his enemy. Dallis had yet to learn why Rory no longer considered Holdenburg a friend. Dallis thought it had something to do with a card game between the late Lord Beckwith and Holdenburg. One where Kathleen might have been part of those stakes. If her guess stood correct, the scandal would ruin Kathleen on a level from which she would never recover.

As Rory fussed, Dallis looked over his shoulder and mouthed the word *later* to the two ladies. They nodded that they understood. She would explain her reasons to them soon.

Rory carried Dallis to the carriage and settled her in the seat. With instructions to the driver to travel at a crawl toward home, he held his wife in his arms. Dallis laid her head on his chest, sighing as he rubbed her stomach. His concern for his wife kept Rory from taking care of his mother and Kathleen's comforts. However, when he heard Holdenburg's name, he paused.

"Did you enjoy your walk with Lord Holdenburg, Kathleen?" his mother asked.

Kathleen blushed and turned to look out the window, answering yes. Not only her blush, but the twisting fingers in her lap gave her away. Rory had heard the duchess ask the same question to Holdenburg at Lord Hartridge's. Why was he left in the dark about Kathleen and Holdenburg's walk? What the hell happened to make his sister so nervous?

"You took a walk with Holdenburg?" Rory asked Kathleen.

Kathleen turned and raised an eyebrow at his tone.

"Yes."

"Alone?"

"No, his footman was present." She denied this too forcefully.

Footman his arse. Rory knew every trick Holdenburg possessed. The footman might have started out with them, but Holdenburg would have dismissed his servant at the first chance he got. Rory ran with the bloke enough in the past to learn every one of his ploys. If Holdenburg thought he could use these on his sister, then he had another thing coming.

Rory eyed his sister. Whenever Holdenburg sniffed around Kathleen again, he would stand guard. The redness of his sister's cheeks spoke volumes.

"From this moment going forward, you will not be left alone with Holdenburg without a chaperone."

"We were not alone, Rory. His servant was present the entire time."

"So, you say, sister. But for my sake of mind, any interaction with Holdenburg will be under my guidance."

"You do not need to worry. There will be no next time, brother."

"Good."

"And why not, dear? You could do worse than Lord Holdenburg," said Lady Beckwith.

"But I could do so much better." Kathleen's voice dripped with sarcasm.

"I do not see why you should not allow Lord Holdenburg to pay court," Dallis chimed in.

Rory looked at his wife in astonishment. Which only caused his mother to grin with approval. The only sane person in this carriage beside himself was Kathleen. She, too, regarded the women as if they were crazy. Rory would have to explain to Dallis the very reason why Holdenburg courting Kathleen would be a recipe for disaster. He had kept this secret from her because they had their own obstacles to overcome. Before Dallis interfered further, Rory must confess his father's greatest sin so she would understand why this could never come to be.

"We went on a walk. There is no courtship involved here."

"But a gentleman taking a lady on a walk *is* a sign of courtship," her mother replied.

"Lord Holdenburg is not courting me, nor do I wish for him to. This discussion is over. My main concern is why Rory carried Dallis to the carriage. Is there something wrong with the babe?"

"Dallis felt ill. I am taking every precaution with her."

Rory pulled Dallis tighter. If anything were to happen to her or the babe, it would devastate him. Dallis was his life. His everything.

"I am fine, only a little nauseous." Dallis sent Mama a look to change the subject. She would explain later her discussion with Sophia and Sidney. Rory's mother wanted Kathleen and Holdenburg to connect. With enough people trying to bring them together, it would be inevitable.

"Rory, dear. Quit smothering the poor girl. She is fine, it is a natural part of pregnancy. She did too much this afternoon. From here on, I will request all meetings to be held at our home. So when Dallis becomes fatigued she can retire to her room."

"I think it would be best, Mama, if Dallis refrains from her charity work until after the babe is born."

"Rory." All three women exclaimed.

"I will be fine, dear husband. If I feel that I cannot continue, then and only then will I bring a halt to my activities. But for now I am perfectly capable of attending a few meetings. I am in the early stages of my pregnancy."

"But your doctor informed us that the first few months are the most important to guard against overtiring yourself."

"In which I have already passed those. I am Scottish, my dear husband, there is not a sturdier woman besides a Scottish woman."

"Unless you're an Irish woman," Kathleen and Mama replied at the same time.

The carriage filled with laughter at the silly notions of their heritages and on who was a stronger woman. Either way, the discussion moved away from Kathleen and Holdenburg. Kathleen must never be left alone with Holdenburg. She sensed that her mother and Dallis intended to play matchmaker between her and the earl. Mama had warned Kathleen that once she had Rory settled in matrimony, Kathleen would be next. Perhaps, in time, Kathleen would search for a groom. But for now she needed to avenge her father's death. Because of Holdenburg, her father passed away a broken man. She didn't have the complete details, but from the tidbits she had overheard, Kathleen knew of his involvement in the final card game that was the start of her father's demise. Holdenburg took everything her father had and caused his heart failure. He stood behind the reason they'd lived in near-poverty for the last few years. She would expose Holdenburg for the devil he was and along the way destroy his reputation. She would make the ton see him for the scoundrel he was. Not a single mama or papa would ever allow him anywhere near their daughters. He would be a pariah.

Chapter Four

The following day Kathleen waited until Rory left for Lord Hartridges' before she snuck into his office. Mama and Dallis were in the nursery, sewing garments for the new babe. They asked her to keep them company, but Kathleen hated the very idea of sewing. Even watching them sew bored her to tears. How women found enjoyment from sewing was a mystery to her.

Kathleen opened the drawers, pulling out letters and replacing them while she hunted for the object that would gain her entry into The Wager. A small token displaying a hand of cards on the front, and on the back were three simple words, Lady Luck's Temptation. Now, where would Rory have hidden his coin? Kathleen knew Rory was in possession of a coin, because it was how he gained entrance into the club to fight.

A brothel located near Vauxhall Gardens had a gaming hell, bar, and fighting club attached to the premises. Where the degenerate lords of London would grace each other's company to drink to excess and gamble away their family's holdings. Then in an underground room of the club was The Scuffle where men battled their disagreements. The owner of this glory was one Madame Bellerose, Belle for short. She ran the entire outfit. Kathleen's father was a frequent visitor and gambled their money away. It was upon her father's death that Rory discovered the depths of their father's depravity. Her brother and mother kept Kathleen shielded from the details of her father's demise, trying to protect her. Rory only visited the establishment to gain their family some extra blunt. He fought bouts to keep the debt collectors at bay. Mama never knew of Rory's fights. Not until after he married Dallis. Only when he came home beaten to a pulp did Rory explain what his outside activities were.

Kathleen had found a coin like the one she searched for now, when Mama gave her a box of her father's things. Mama thought she would enjoy having a few trinkets to remember Papa by, mementos of her father. Contained inside the box was a deck of cards they used when they played whist. When Kathleen dumped the deck onto the bed, a token slid out. She flipped it over and over, trying to discover the purpose behind the token. She stared at it for hours, imagining what Papa used it for. Frustrated, she delved into the box searching for any more clues to what it might be for, and she came across a promissory note. It was a receipt for a large sum of money that Papa owed to none other than Devon Holdenburg. Included on the receipt was the name of the establishment where Papa lost his money. The Wager.

So, Kathleen, naïve that she was, attempted to gain entry with the coin, only to be refused at the door. A giant of a man commanded the doorway, regarding her with indifference before he took the coin and slammed the door in her face. Kathleen didn't know if his refusal had anything to do with her dressing like a boy and looking like a young pup trying to gain entry into the gaming hell. Either way, the brute never answered after she pounded on the door for half an hour. Feeling bummed, Kathleen kicked the door one last time and wandered down the alley. When she'd heard the rumble of carriage wheels, Kathleen peeked around the corner, watching two gentlemen exit their carriage and proceed to the door. The door opened to them, and they flashed their tokens. When the guard looked the tokens over and they passed inspection, the gentlemen gained access to the establishment. Kathleen stayed in the shadows, watching the comings and goings for the remainder of the afternoon. She observed the many ladies and gentlemen who visited. Masks, hoods, or veils hid the ladies' identities. Kathleen gained a sense of how she needed to proceed with her plan. She'd acted rashly before realizing the bigger picture. Kathleen continued home to alter her strategy to make Devon Holdenburg pay for her father's demise.

This was how she came to be searching in her brother's study for a coin to begin her revenge. At that moment, Kathleen realized Rory wouldn't hide the coin in his office, and she had an idea where the coin might be. When they were younger, and Rory wanted to hide his treats or toys from Kathleen, he would put them in a secret place. It wasn't until Kathleen became older that she discovered Rory hid them in plain sight. She would search everywhere for them, only to find his hiding places were in the nursery where she played.

The token must be in the nursery.

Kathleen hurried to the nursery. She ran upstairs, excited with the knowledge on where the token might be. Reaching the room, Kathleen came to a halt when she overheard her name mentioned. Not only her name, but that scoundrel, Holdenburg too.

"They would be perfect for each other."

"I agree, dear. But they have many obstacles to overcome before their relationship can flourish," Mama said.

"Yes, I understand. Rory forbids Holdenburg anywhere near Kathleen. While I don't agree with my husband, Holdenburg still has his work cut out for him."

"Yes, I explained to Devon that he would need to show patience with Kathleen. But he fears Kathleen's anger towards him will never diminish," Mama said.

"My heart goes out to him. I wish him the best of luck and I will aid him in any way I can. His offer of friendship during our courtship endeared him to me."

"I am truly sorry for that ordeal, my dear. Holdenburg holds guilt over one of my late husband's indiscretions. While I never faulted Devon, I took advantage of him by asking him to court you. I only meant to draw my son toward you. In the end, it all worked out fine."

Dallis laughed. "Yes, it did. What are our plans for throwing those two together? Sophia and Sidney wish to help."

"Yes, I thought they might. The duchess also wishes for Devon and Kathleen to make a match. She knows her son yearns for my daughter and is more than pleased to offer assistance in any way she can."

"Well, with all this help, Devon should be able to charm Kathleen off her feet in no time. Do you know what his next move might be?"

"He plans to …"

"Please excuse me, Lady Kathleen." The maid spoke from behind Kathleen.

"Kathleen, dear. Have you decided to join us after all?" Mama asked.

Kathleen tamped down her annoyance while she followed the maid into the room with the tea tray. They meant to throw Kathleen at Holdenburg's feet. Over her dead body. There was no way she would succumb to his charm. And to think they were her family. Kathleen should have known better. She had watched her mother's devious tricks when trying to match Rory with Dallis.

With a calm face Kathleen replied, "Yes, Mama. I thought I would rearrange the books and toys on the shelves for the baby. It has been awhile and some toys need to be repaired or thrown away."

"What an excellent idea. I was just reminiscing with Dallis about the wonderful times you children shared in this nursery."

"Oh, were you now?" Kathleen muttered under her breath.

"Remember the time, Kathleen, when Rory and Devon hid behind the curtains while you were playing with your dolls. Then the boys started making strange noises and whispering your name. You ran to your father's study, shaking in fright. He carried you upstairs, trying to calm your fears by telling you there were no such things as ghosts. Your cries only grew louder the closer you came to the nursery. I rushed above stairs and you held onto my skirts when father went in to inspect the room. And there behind the curtains, Rory and Devon rolled around on the floor, laughing on how they scared you."

"Yes, and then Papa, my hero, grabbed both boys by the ears and scolded them something fierce. Then he made them play dolls with me for the rest of the afternoon. They had to follow whatever I wanted to do. When they tried to sneak away, Father sat in the rocking chair, reading his book, making them obey his wishes."

"There were never more two miserable boys than that afternoon. I do believe after that day they never picked on you again."

"So they would have led you to believe, Mother."

"Yes, they were ornery. Still are, I think."

"Mmm." Was the only reply Kathleen would allow her mother.

Kathleen picked up her cup of tea and carried it across the room to where the books rested. She'd learned Rory had a secret book where he hid smaller items. He hollowed out a book with a gory title. Anything gothic always scared Kathleen, so she avoided these. She only discovered the mystery when it fell to the floor while she tried to pull out a book she wanted. When the book fell open, her brother's treasures spilled out. They were his toy soldiers that Father had taken away from him for being naughty, because Rory wouldn't share with Kathleen. Rory had stolen them back and hid them away in the book.

Since Rory wasn't at home, Kathleen had played with the toy soldiers during the afternoon before she put them away. She pretended to be innocent of his hiding place and every time he wasn't around, she would open the book to discover what new treasure he hid away. Every toy she played with, without his knowledge. When Rory hid candy, she would sneak a piece for herself. Kathleen smiled to herself with these memories. She sipped her tea as she read the titles of the books. The same titles Rory would read to her on rainy afternoons. He was an indulgent older brother. Although there were the times Rory pretended she was a nuisance, especially when Holdenburg was present, for the most part he was the best brother any girl could ever have.

She would repay his kindness with her own, with his children. She planned on doting on her niece or nephew when they were born. Kathleen's excitement mirrored Rory and Dallis's happiness for a new baby in the house.

Kathleen moved a book here and there while she searched. She wanted to portray to Mama and Dallis that she was indeed organizing, even though she searched more than anything else.

When her fingers pulled the next tome out, Kathleen found what she searched for. The book was light and gave a tinkling sound as something slid back and forth inside. With a glance over her shoulder, she saw Mama and Dallis with their heads bent together, admiring the fabric of a quilt.

Kathleen opened the book. What she searched for laid resting inside. A token. However, it was a different color than her father's. This one was red and on the front were two boxers inside a ring. Whereas her father's coin had been green and depicted a hand of cards. Kathleen didn't think the different coin would matter when she presented it to the guard. Especially when the next time she arrived, Kathleen would be dressed as a lady in disguise. Once she presented the token, Kathleen held faith she would be permitted to enter. Kathleen hid the coin inside the folds of her dress. Sliding the book back into place, Kathleen continued to straighten the titles. She then moved onto the toys to inspect them. Kathleen didn't want to draw any suspicious attention. Once she finished, Kathleen joined the ladies to discuss further plans for the nursery. A smile of satisfaction graced Kathleen's face when she realized she could start her plan of action into play this evening.

After the Camville Ball.

Chapter Five

Devon searched the ball for Kathleen. He'd obtained knowledge on good authority that she would be present this evening. He must proceed with caution. After the park, Devon knew he confused Kathleen. Tonight would be different. Devon would act the perfect gentleman, even if it took everything out of him. He needed to charm Kathleen. Why was it so bloody hard with her? With the other silly debutantes or old matrons, it came easy. Especially the widows, he never had a problem charming them. But Lady Kathleen Beckwith was different.

He found her. She stood next to her family, talking with Dallis. Her face lit up with a smile. She looked lovely. Lovely was too soft a word. She was magnificent. Her long luxurious black hair was bound in curls atop her head. Pearls were interwoven between the strands, making them shine. Her gown of pale pink flowed around her body. But the fabric wrapped around her middle gave him pause. A dark sapphire-blue ribbon graced her narrow waist. Did she wear it for him? Could he hope that pursuing Kathleen would be easier than he thought?

His eyes continued their perusal clear down to her slippers and back up again. The bodice of her dress was prim and proper, and tight. While a gentleman couldn't look down her dress, it left the imagination plenty. Silk tightly encased her breasts. The shape of them leaving many wondering what charms lay underneath her virgin pink. Holdenburg remembered the pleasure of caressing them. If he brushed his thumbs across her nipples right now, would they harden? What shade of pink were her buds? He ached to stroke his tongue across them. His pants tightened, and he realized he needed to rein in his thoughts. It wouldn't do to become aroused in the middle of a ball. Not when he tried to play down his scoundrel image.

Devon sighed and walked outside for a breath of fresh air before he made his way to Kathleen. Leaning over the balcony, he drew in a deep breath. After he brought his body under control, he turned to make his way back inside. However, he was halted by the very man he hated more than anybody he knew. Lord Velden.

Devon already knew what the overbearing ass would ask. Hell would have to freeze over before Devon gave into the lord's request.

"I see the lady of your winnings is present this evening. Such a lovely creature. I might request her hand for a dance."

Devon remained calm and tried not to rise to Lord Velden's comments.

"What do you want, Velden?"

"A chance to replay our game. That way I don't have to play this cat-and-mouse game of courtship with Lady Kathleen. I have decided I still wish for her to be mine. And if my sources are correct, then her brother would approve of the match, considering their financial situation."

"Your sources are wrong. With Beckwith's marriage to Lady Dallis MacPherson, their family is stable. And you are forgetting one detail."

"And that would be?"

"Beckwith is well aware of all the players involved in the game with his father and he would not let you pursue his sister."

"Yes, well, what the brother doesn't know until it is too late won't hurt him."

"Lady Kathleen would never give you the time of day."

"It would appear you have gained no favors with her yourself. Anyway, I like a challenge. And she seems like she would be worth the extra effort."

Devon could do one of two things. He could threaten Lord Velden, which would only entice the man to chase Kathleen more. Or he could pretend indifference and hope Velden ceased his pursuit. Either way, Devon was damned. Lord Velden would no more abandon his plan until he achieved his goals, than Holdenburg could control his temper.

"Do not go anywhere near her," Devon growled.

"And if I do?"

"Then I shall destroy you. Which I should have done that night."

Lord Velden laughed. "Then the card game is a no?"

Devon scowled and stalked into the ballroom. The lord's comment didn't warrant an answer.

Devon noticed Kathleen standing next to a gaggle of girls and approached her for a dance. He should wait for his temper to calm, but the fear of Lord Velden requesting a dance from Kathleen prompted him to hurry.

This ball bored Kathleen to tears. The young debutantes, whispering in the corner about the scandalous lords they wished to ask them to dance, grated on her nerves. The silly chits didn't realize those lords would only ruin them in the gardens. Those gentlemen never danced, only seduced. Even the very lord who stalked towards her. She needed to avoid him at all costs. The more time she spent in his company, the more she fell for his charm. But she was too late.

Devon saw Kathleen trying to run from him, only there was nowhere for her to go. He had her trapped. The pale pink of Kathleen's gown blended in with the other girls, but the dark blue sapphire ribbon tied around her waist stood out in a crowd. Devon saw it as a sign of Kathleen's devotion to please him.

"You look like a swirl of pink candy in your dress, Lady Kathleen. I am honored by your choice to please me with your ribbon."

"Wipe the smug smile from your face, my lord. My mother left me no choice. It was either wear this ribbon or help cook scour pots. You can see which choice I have taken."

"All the same, it pleases me greatly."

Kathleen chose not to respond. Let Holdenburg believe what he wanted to; it made no difference to her.

"May I ask for your hand in the next set?"

"I am sorry, my lord, my dance card is full." Kathleen held the card for him to see.

"My unfortunate luck for not requesting sooner. I hope you enjoy your evening, my lady."

Kathleen felt disappointment when he didn't linger to bait her like he normally did. When he continued onto the simple misses and asked one of them for a dance, Kathleen frowned. Why did she let herself believe that his request for a dance was special? Maybe because it was his first attempt.

When Kathleen's dance partner approached, they moved to the center of the ballroom floor. Once the music started, Kathleen saw she would have to dance along with Holdenburg. The first twirl around he never spoke, only holding her hand as they moved amongst the dancers. On the next turn, his fingers caressed hers. Each twirl enticed her to his seduction.

On the final twirl, he whispered, "You look sweet enough to taste."

Kathleen tripped, and Holdenburg steadied her, never missing a step, passing Kathleen off to her partner. After the dance concluded, Holdenburg escorted his partner onto the terrace. It would seem the silly twit got her dance from a scoundrel, now she would get her ruination. Kathleen followed them, but the pressing crowd held her back. When she finally made her way onto the balcony, Kathleen found it deserted. Holdenburg must have lured the girl into the gardens.

Kathleen continued down the stairs and along the well-lit path. With each turn of the maze, she ventured deeper into the darkness. She couldn't find them. When Kathleen came to the middle of the maze, she found Holdenburg lounging on a bench by the fountain. Alone. No innocent miss held in his clutches. Kathleen didn't know whether to feel relieved or angry. She wanted to find him deflowering an innocent to prove to her mother and Dallis his scandalous nature. Both women thought him a saint and bowed to his charm. However, Kathleen knew different. Rory knew the man to be a ruthless scoundrel and kept her away from him. Now she was alone with him in the middle of the garden. Kathleen didn't want to understand why she felt relief. Her emotions rose too close to the surface.

The darkness only emphasized his masculinity. The shadows played tricks on her imagination. Holdenburg sat with one leg propped on the bench with his elbow hanging across his knee and his hand dangling in mid-air. Nonchalant, so very like the man himself. His dark suit blended in, but the starkness of his cream-colored cravat stood out. A lit cigar dangled between his fingers, the smoke curling in the air. He lifted it to his mouth and took a long drag. Holdenburg didn't speak, just watched Kathleen, waiting for her insults.

Kathleen didn't know if it was the privacy of the garden or his sensual gaze that lowered her inhibitions. Perhaps it was his whispered words from the dance. They held the same effect as his kisses in the park. Each time enticing her to explore the passion radiating off him.

Devon watched the conflicting emotions cross Kathleen's face. Every time he was near her, he meant to play the consummate gentleman with her, but she enflamed his senses into acting the scoundrel she believed him to be.

Kathleen should run back to the house as far away from him as she could, but she stayed rooted to the spot. Holdenburg needed to scare her away. He meant to make her his, but not in this manner. Not where the ton forced their hand. When Kathleen became his, it would be because he wore down the last of her resistance.

"Did you come to fulfill my request?" he asked.

"Your request?"

"I wish to taste your sweet confection."

"You sir, are most improper."

"And you, my lady, are a temptation I wish not to deny myself."

"You make no sense in your utter ramblings."

Devon pushed himself off the bench and snuffed the cigar, strolling to her side.

"Then let me make myself clear, where your innocent ears can understand what I am saying. I wish to taste you. First, I would start on your lips, for they are the sweetest temptation. Then I would trail my mouth to your breasts and suck your pebbles until they harden under my tongue. When I had my fill, I would continue between your legs where—"

Kathleen slapped him across the face. A resounding smack echoing in the night air. She gasped and stepped back. Kathleen couldn't believe she'd struck Devon. Her eyes widened as Devon scowled and advanced toward Kathleen. She turned and ran. Ran as fast as her legs would carry her, which wasn't far. Her breath loud in her ears, Kathleen heard Devon catching up. Her skirts became tangled and Kathleen was no match for Devon.

Devon grabbed Kathleen from behind and held her in an iron embrace. He pulled her closer. Kathleen struggled to get free, but Devon's arms only tightened more. His warm breath brushed across her neck.

"I will allow you that act only once, my lady. The next time your hand touches me, it will be in pleasure. If you were a man, I would call you out. Instead I will extract my own revenge on your senses."

"Never," Kathleen hissed.

"Never is a long time, my dear."

"Unhand me, this once."

"No, I think I will take my revenge now."

Devon's lips brushed across her neck in a caress so soft, Kathleen thought she imagined it. She whimpered from the unknown. When Devon tipped her head back and took her lips in a kiss meant to destroy her, he surprised Kathleen. She expected Devon's anger from his kiss, instead the caress was gentle. So gentle, Kathleen melted into him. She sighed as his tongue enticed her lips to part. When Kathleen opened to him, Devon overtook her senses. He loosened his hold and turned her around in his arms. His kiss awakened her to his passion. Every nip and stroke of Devon's tongue urged her to succumb. As soon as Kathleen responded, Devon stopped. Stepping away, he regarded her with his usual smug expression.

"Your *never* did not last very long."

Kathleen raised her hand to slap him again. He grabbed her wrist, his touch as gentle as his kiss.

"Remember my threat."

Devon dropped her hand, walking away from Kathleen, back into the darkness of the garden. Kathleen rubbed her wrist. His words and actions contradicted each other. She knew she crossed a line with slapping him. It was only because Devon's whispered words shocked her. Not only shocked Kathleen, but aroused her. She should have never shown Devon her displeasure. It was the number one rule in any game. You never showed your opponent your emotions.

The touch of Devon's lips still tingled. Kathleen expected his anger when he'd grabbed her. She was unprepared for Devon's gentle caress. His exploration of her mouth exploded her senses. Then when Kathleen tried to slap him, Devon only displayed patience with her. Lord Holdenburg remained more of a mystery than ever before.

Devon continued walking away until he was out of sight, taking him deeper into the garden where other couples snuck away for secret trysts. Devon's need for Kathleen consumed his senses, and he didn't notice the gentleman leaning against the tree. The first taste of Kathleen's lips had heightened his senses to a level he'd never known. Devon knew Kathleen expected anger from her slap, but while he enjoyed their barbs, Devon could never hurt her. Kathleen was more precious to him than anything in the world. Never would Devon raise a hand to harm her. Kathleen was meant for loving. It was only a matter of time before Kathleen would be his.

Kathleen tried to return to the party but got lost in the twists and turns of the maze. She paused at another dead end. With a hitch in her breath,

Kathleen tried to keep her anxiety from taking over. The whispers of the night echoed all around. The darkness closed in. When Kathleen stood on her tiptoes, the lights from the house seemed farther in the distance. Somehow, she had retreated to the back of the maze. After taking many deep breaths, Kathleen's nerves calmed. That was until she heard the shuffling of feet coming closer.

Kathleen's eyes darted, looking for a place to hide. She didn't want anybody to see what a fool she had been by getting lost. Also, if it were a gentleman, then Kathleen risked being caught in a compromising situation. But there was nowhere to go. She was trapped. Perhaps, if Kathleen squeezed between the hedges, she would go unnoticed. As the dark shadow grew closer, Kathleen tried to wedge herself in between the thorny vines, but their sharpness prevented her. If she continued, she would rip her dress, and that would draw too much attention.

Kathleen decided to play on her acting skills. Her greatest desire was to be on the stage, but she couldn't because of her status in the ton. That didn't stop her from acting now.

With her head bent, she walked closer to the shadow and began to cry. By the time Kathleen bumped into the shadow, tears streamed along her cheeks.

Hands steadied Kathleen. When fingers covered in gloves lifted her head, Kathleen encountered a set of haunting eyes. His dark gaze pierced her soul with a blackness that couldn't be explained. The kind that sent a chill running along Kathleen's back. However, the gentleman's smile suggested someone entirely different. It held compassion as his fingers wiped the tears from her face.

His gentle voice calmed her fears where she'd thought her overactive imagination convinced her he was somebody dark and sinister.

"Now, now, my dear, it cannot be as awful as all this fuss."

Kathleen managed a hiccup to top off her dramatic act. "I fear I am lost and have no direction on how to leave this confusing maze."

"Perhaps I can be of assistance? I only came outside for some fresh air to escape the stifling heat of the ballroom."

"I do not wish to take you away from your peace of mind."

"But I will no longer be at peace if I neglect to aid a charming lady in her confusion. Shall we?"

His smile urged her to agree. Kathleen must have imagined the evil in his eyes when they first came into contact. For he had shown nothing but a true gentleman's character. He didn't force himself on Kathleen and take advantage of her virtue.

Kathleen slipped a hand under his arm as he guided them along the path. As he negotiated the many twists and turns, Kathleen saw the lights beckoning them were closer.

"If I may be so bold, my lady, my name is Lord Velden."

"Your boldness is most welcome. I should apologize for not offering my name. I am Lady Kathleen Beckwith."

Lord Velden still smiled at her. "It is a pleasure to make your acquaintance, Lady Kathleen."

"The pleasure is all mine. I do not know how I can ever repay your kindness for escorting me out of this madness they call a maze."

Lord Velden laughed. His laughter gave Kathleen the same discomfort from when she first encountered his gaze. However, his touch remained impersonal and didn't step over the bounds of impropriety. Lord Velden continued to act as if he only set about a good deed. Kathleen's imagination had to be playing tricks, conjuring falsehoods. Her confrontation with Holdenburg had left Kathleen emotional and allowed her confusion to interfere with Lord Velden.

"I know it would be very unladylike of me to ask, but can I repay your kindness with a dance?"

"Your offer is very tempting, my lady. But I must decline. I must attend a prior engagement that I am late for. Perhaps I can accept your repayment in another form?"

"Oh," Kathleen paused, pulling her hand away.

"Nothing as nefarious as that. I thought more along the line of your attendance as my guest at the theater next week."

"I am sorry, but I must decline."

"Yes, that was too presumptuous of me."

"No, it was a grand offer. However, my mother has already accepted an offer from Lord Holdenburg. Perhaps we will see each other there?"

"Yes, perhaps."

Lord Velden bowed and lifted her gloved hand, placing a kiss across her knuckles.

"Until we meet again, my lady. The minutes spent apart will only enhance our time to come."

With those romantic words, Lord Velden escaped into the night. Kathleen sighed from his seductive goodbye. He'd acted the perfect gentleman during her rescue. Kathleen stood at the entrance, alone. She could enter the ball without detection and not have to answer to her whereabouts. If questioned, Kathleen would weave a story about a friend's tragic encounter with a scoundrel.

Chapter Six

Holdenburg saw Kathleen enter the ballroom through the terrace doors with a group of partygoers. The dreamy expression on her face brought forth a scowl. When Holdenburg left Kathleen in the maze, a look of shock had graced her. Now Kathleen appeared as if she held a secret bringing much pleasure. When Holdenburg had finally regretted his actions he went after Kathleen, only to find no trace of her in the maze. After he worked his way out, Holdenburg continued to the ballroom to offer his apologies. However, Kathleen wasn't there either. Holdenburg searched everywhere.

When he couldn't locate her, Holdenburg inquired to Kathleen's whereabouts with her family. All that did was to draw attention to Kathleen's absence. Holdenburg never meant to give them a reason for concern. Kathleen's family dispersed trying to find her safe before word spread of her disappearance.

Holdenburg strode to Kathleen's side, separating her from the crowd and guiding her behind the columns.

"Where have you been?" Holdenburg demanded.

Kathleen jerked herself away. She wiped her palms along the folds of her dress, hiding their shaking. This evening had developed into a scene from one of the dramas she enjoyed watching. Lord Velden's goodbye still shook her with a temptation that she wished to explore. With the reappearance of Holdenburg, Kathleen grew more confused than ever. His high-handiness infuriated her, yet she could hear the concern in his voice. She would have responded to his fear, but her anger at his earlier actions prompted her to reply sharply.

"Where or who I was with is of no concern of yours. You are not my keeper, nor will you ever be." Kathleen tried to step around Holdenburg, and he blocked her path.

"Your every action is my concern, or will be soon." Holdenburg made his threat be known before he stepped away. He made to turn when he halted, recalling Kathleen's objection. *Who I was with?* What did she imply?

"You were not alone in the garden? Who did you keep company with?"

Kathleen closed her mouth, shocked at Holdenburg's mention of being her keeper soon. Kathleen didn't want to divulge the name of her rescuer. It would be her secret. If Lord Velden never entered her life again, then their time would only be a moment in the darkness of night that drew out her curiosity. If she saw Lord Velden once more, then Kathleen would know he held interest in her company. Her lips tightened at the storm in Holdenburg's eyes. Kathleen took a step back, and Holdenburg followed.

"Who was he?" Holdenburg growled.

"Who said it was a gentleman?"

"The dreamy look on your face at the mere mention that you were not alone."

Kathleen had betrayed herself. Now she must convince Holdenburg that she wasn't alone with a man.

"Fine, for your information I was consoling Lady Madeline. That scoundrel Lord Millard led her away to the gardens. He attempted to seduce her innocence away. When I came across her, I could not leave her alone. I listened to her sad tale and helped to repair her appearance. Then once she calmed enough to return, we blended in with the crowd returning to the ballroom."

Devon listened to her long-winded excuse. Did Kathleen think she could fool him into believing this nonsense? He leaned over to whisper in her ear.

"Do not think for one second your acting has fooled me. I know your true nature, my dear. Your story is false, but you may fool your family with this performance once they ask for your explanation. I, on the other hand, will seek my answer another way."

"What way?" Kathleen squeaked, backing against the wall.

Devon smiled as he reached to run his thumb across her quivering lips. Yes, he knew Kathleen lied, but she could keep her little secret for now. He would make sure to have Kathleen within his sight at future gatherings. But before he left her, Devon wanted to leave Kathleen with a different memory from the disastrous one of before.

Kathleen's lips opened under the gentle stroking. Devon lowered his head and kissed Kathleen with a passion to leave her clinging to his shoulders. He wanted to enflame her senses with nothing but memories of him. The need to wipe away Kathleen's secret encounter drew him to crush her lips under his and stake his claim. When she whimpered and opened her mouth under his, Devon no longer held back. He stole kiss after kiss from her, leaving her wondering of the passion they could share. As he pulled away, his thumb stroked the wetness off her lips.

"You will have to wait and find out."

With those last words he sauntered away. It was one of the hardest things he did this evening. But if he were to stay, then Kathleen would experience what it felt like to be scandalously seduced in a crowded ballroom. Devon took himself discreetly away, waiting for Kathleen to emerge from behind the columns. When she emerged, Kathleen appeared composed except for one small detail. A look filled with desire now replaced Kathleen's dreamy expression. The only thing that held him back from rejoining her was when she lifted her hands to her lips and they shook. A sense of smugness settled over him once he realized Kathleen wasn't as indifferent to him as she portrayed. He blended into the crowd once Dallis approached Kathleen. She would be safe now that her family found her. Devon needed to leave before he did anything else foolish this evening.

Dallis approached a stunned Kathleen emerging from behind a set of columns. She wrapped her arms around Kathleen's waist as she drew her away. Dallis looked over her shoulder for anybody hidden in the darkness. When Dallis couldn't see anybody, she focused on her sister-in-law. Dallis had never seen Kathleen in this state before and grew concerned, especially after Holdenburg had noted her disappearance. Dallis remembered, not so long ago, her own experience of being whisked away behind columns at a ball. Unfortunately for her, nothing happened. That was not without wishing something would have. Not that it mattered anymore, because her scoundrel finally ruined her into the happiest of marriages.

Regardless, it would appear Kathleen *had* encountered somebody.

"Kathleen, what has happened?"

"His kiss," she muttered.

"His kiss? Kathleen, who kissed you?" Dallis whispered before Rory and Mama appeared.

"Kathleen, where were you?" Mama asked.

Dallis watched the transformation in Kathleen. No longer was she the stunned debutante, but an actress who strung together a story to fool her family. Dallis recalled acting this way with her grandmother and knew a storyteller when she saw one. The only thing making Kathleen more believable was her acting skills. Kathleen adored the theater and thought herself an actress. Dallis knew there was more to Kathleen's story than she let on. Dallis wouldn't interfere for now. But once she got a moment alone with Kathleen, she would get her answers.

~~~~~

Kathleen settled under the covers while her maid, Susan, put her clothes away. She had adjustments to make with having a maid once more. After her father passed away, money had been too tight for extra servants. During that time Kathleen had come to enjoy her privacy and independence. Since Dallis and Rory had married, Dallis's money provided them with the privilege to employ more servants. Kathleen tried to refuse, knowing a maid would be one more person she needed to sneak away from.

After Susan left, Kathleen rose quietly from the bed and pulled out the dress she bought with secret pin money. Part of her felt guilty for keeping this money hidden while their family suffered financially. She'd never spent the extra coin in case she would need to return them to Rory. But luckily, she never had to. Once Dallis shared her wealth, the guilt subsided, and Kathleen commissioned the dress. Oh, not from their regular dress maker, but from one she overheard at a party. Someone who doesn't question anything but the coin you paid with.

Kathleen had poured over the designer's fashion plates until she found the dress that would present her as a lady of rich standing. The one thing she requested was the placement of the fastenings on the gown. Kathleen instructed the dressmaker to hide them in the front, decorated by jewels. That way she could dress herself in the creation without the help of any maid.

Since Susan was a new servant, Kathleen didn't know if she could trust her. Probably not, since the girl's loyalty laid with whom provided her pay. Rory.

Kathleen drew off her nightgown and slid the new silk creation up her body. She decided to forgo a corset and only wore a thin chemise. The gown was a deep scarlet that enhanced the color of her hair. As Kathleen slid the buttons together, she took a deep breath when the gown tightened around her chest. When she looked in the mirror, she noticed her breasts spilled forth from the gown. Kathleen's first instinct was to grab a shawl to cover herself, but she stopped. The woman who stared back from the mirror was unknown. The boldness of the lady took pride in her sensuality. Was that image really her? Kathleen held her head higher and confidence shone from the light in her eyes. She raised her hands and ran them along the sides of her breasts, then across her waist. As Kathleen touched herself, thoughts of Devon Holdenburg invaded her senses. How would his hands feel caressing her like this? Would his lips follow the trail of his hands?

Kathleen shook her head to stop. She didn't have time for this foolishness. Kathleen must stop thinking of Devon's kisses. They were moments best forgotten. Devon was a scoundrel who only toyed with her emotions. Kathleen's revenge toward Devon would come later. For now, she needed to gain access to the gaming hell.

Kathleen located the reticule she had fashioned like her dress and opened it to check the token resting inside. Also, there were a few bills to get her started. She would win more later to continue playing. Kathleen slipped on the black gloves to finish her ensemble. Once she arrived at the gaming hell, she would ask for a mask to hide her identity. Kathleen heard that was how a lady of the ton could remain anonymous inside the establishment.

Opening the door, Kathleen listened for any noise to delay her departure. She looked along the hallway and saw no light shining from under the doors. Kathleen worked her way down the servant's backstairs. Outside, she walked briskly to the alley to where a hackney waited. Secure and with directions to her destination, Kathleen relaxed. The first stage to this evening was a success. She had escaped with no one the wiser.

Chapter Seven

Kathleen knocked and waited for the door to open. The same guard opened the door. He scowled. She never wavered under the brute's stare. To most he would intimidate them with his size and the tattoo upon his arm. The sheer size of him alone would frighten most women. That didn't deter Kathleen. She opened the reticule and withdrew the token. She passed it to him under the dim light coming from inside. He flipped the coin over and then glared at Kathleen. The giant looked her up and down before allowing her inside. His gruff voice demanded that Kathleen follow him.

He led Kathleen down a darkened hallway and into an elegant parlor. This wasn't a parlor Kathleen expected to find in a brothel.

"Madame likes to welcome any new members to the establishment. She will attend to you shortly."

"Thank you, sir."

The giant paused as Kathleen paid him the respect he deserved. After standing there for endless moments, his glance took in her full appearance. He nodded his approval before he took his leave.

Kathleen moved to the sofa and sat poised, waiting for the Madame to show. She wished to explore the room, but didn't want to appear like a sneak. Kathleen wanted to present herself as a member of the highest society. To achieve this, she mustn't show interest of something as simple as a parlor.

~~~~~

Ned brought the token to his mistress, tossing it on the desk. Belle looked up from some paperwork, arching an eyebrow in question.

"Do you remember the street urchin from last week?"

"The one who tried to enter with the late Lord Beckwith's coin?"

"The same. She has returned and presented this coin but has changed her appearance to a lady."

"This is Rory's coin."

"Yes."

"Interesting. Where might I find this creature?"

"I have inserted her in your visiting parlor. I explained how you wished to greet new members."

"Perfect. Thank you, Ned, that will be all. After I talk with her, I will inform you of her membership and what precautions we may need to take."

"Very well," he answered, returning to his duties.

Belle relaxed back in the chair, flipping the coin between her fingers. What an interesting development. How to proceed? With both coins belonging to the men of the Beckwith household, she could only be one lady. Lady Kathleen Beckwith. The word surrounding the lady was one of a spoiled debutante. Spoiled? Or was the chit confident of what she desired and would never accept no for an answer? She could deny the girl access to the establishment, or she could open the doors. Either way it would be a tricky situation. It would appear the girl had a purpose for trying to enter and wouldn't be put off. It would be best to gauge the reason and then explore the options.

~~~~~~

The door opened to the parlor with an exotic beauty entering, followed by a maid carrying a tea tray. The woman gave directions and waited until the maid left before addressing Kathleen.

Kathleen sat in awe as the woman before her dominated the room with an arrogance Kathleen had only witnessed from men. Kathleen thought her own scarlet dress to be scandalous, but it was nothing compared to the creation molded to the lady's body. The dark green fabric clung to the woman's curves, her breasts on full display, the pearls decorating the edge of the dress barely hiding her nipples. The dress appeared to only cling tighter around her legs and buttocks. Kathleen gawked at the open display of femininity. Kathleen had heard rumors of Madame Bellerose. None of them compared to meeting the lady in person. Most women this beautiful held a smug arrogance to their charms, and Kathleen was unprepared for the kindness the lady displayed. Her smile contained warmth and openness when she reached for Kathleen's hands, gently squeezing them before she settled across from her.

"May I inquire to whom I have the honor of greeting?"

"I prefer not to give my name. I wish to hide my identity. You may call me Scarlet."

"I am Madame Bellerose. All my friends call me Belle. I feel this is the start of a budding friendship."

Kathleen didn't answer Madame Bellerose's declaration. She'd hardly thought to be friends with the Madame of a brothel. Since Kathleen didn't want to offend the lady, she only nodded.

Belle held back a smirk. She took no offense. While most ladies never form a friendship with someone of Belle's standing, they always ended up sharing more with her than they originally thought.

"Would you like some tea, my lady? Or perhaps something a little stronger. I have a sweet madeira I have been meaning to try."

"A glass of madeira would be lovely."

Belle rose and poured each of them a glass of wine. As she drank, Belle assessed the young lady. Belle had yet to understand the reason for Lady Kathleen's arrival and wondered if perhaps the lady sought companionship. Belle was told on good authority that Rory's financials had taken an upward swing. So, money couldn't be the purpose of Lady Kathleen's appearance. However, the dress the lady wore spoke otherwise. It ranked alongside Belle's own scandalous outfit. If the lady *wasn't* trying to display her assets, Belle was clueless to her motives.

Kathleen sipped the wine while the Madame scrutinized her. She wondered if she passed inspection. When the silence continued, Kathleen took a deeper gulp of wine, her confidence wavering.

"What is the pleasure you seek?" Belle asked.

"Pleasure?"

"Yes, pleasure." Belle didn't go into detail of the many pleasures one could find in her establishment.

"I think you misunderstand why I am here."

"Perhaps you can clarify."

"I seek your card rooms. The rumors whispered around in the ballrooms is that your gaming hell is the best in London. I wish to play cards."

"To play cards in my gaming hell, you must be a member. There are only two ways to gain membership."

"But I am already a member, I presented my token at the entrance."

"Tis not your token, my lady."

"A friend offered their coin to me in exchange for a favor."

"I do not abide lies in my club."

"I do not lie."

"If you cannot be honest with me, then I will have Ned escort you to the door. The next time you attempt to enter, it will not be as pleasant as this meeting."

"But my token?"

"The token you presented belongs to a member who has withdrawn his membership. Also, if you looked over the token, you would have noticed that the token displayed fighters. That token would only gain you access to the fighting arena and nowhere else. The other token you presented a few weeks ago, dressed as a boy, belonged to a member who has since passed away. Now *that* coin would have gained you entry to the gaming hell and the brothel. Since both coins belonged to members of the same family, I conclude that you are the sister and daughter of the owners of the previous coins. Am I correct?"

"Yes." Kathleen sighed. Her confidence no longer wavered, it had now vanished.

"I'm glad that matter is settled. I detest liars. Now, hiding the truth to protect somebody, that is a different reason. Do you understand?"

"Yes, I understand."

"Excellent. Now, what is your pleasure?"

"Excuse me?"

"With your presentation of both coins, it opens your options wider. Fighting, cards, or the brothel. Perhaps all three?" Belle arched one eyebrow, the look in her eyes tempting Kathleen to all three choices.

Kathleen's blush of innocence betrayed the sophistication she attempted to display. However, she couldn't control it. Her sheltered upbringing conflicted with the temptations held before her. Did Devon visit the brothel? *Devon?* Why did she address him as Devon now? Kathleen knew why, but kept trying to deny her reasons for keeping those thoughts at bay. Devon's kisses this evening had opened a floodgate of emotions. He had always been 'Devon' to her and always would be. Even when she became wed to another, he would hold a special place in her heart. If only Kathleen held the same place in his. But throughout the years she'd watched Devon seduce one lady after another and knew it would never be her. Even watching Devon court Dallis a few months ago pierced her heart. Kathleen watched how his eyes softened around Dallis when he tried to protect her from Rory's ungentlemanly behavior. Kathleen tried not succumbing to jealousy over their bond of friendship, but it was of no use. When Rory had finally dug his head out of his arse and professed his love to Dallis, then and only then did Kathleen feel relieved. However, it would be short-lived. Because once again Devon Holdenburg remained out of her reach. Kathleen watched how he strolled the ballroom floor searching for his next conquest. Devon's seductive smile drew every lady to his side. Devon turned his smile on everybody but her. Until this evening.

"Your card room is all that I require."

"Now, as I stated before, you can gain membership one of two ways. You can either have a long-standing member sponsor your entrance, or else I can sponsor your membership. Do you have anyone you can ask to sponsor you?"

Kathleen had nobody she wished to know of her activities. Not that anybody would sponsor her anyway. That only left her to persuade the Madame into sponsoring her. She shook her head.

"As I thought. The only way that I would entertain supporting your cause would be to hear your story. Please explain to me why a lady of your standing would want to subject herself to ruin for the sake of a game of cards?"

"I wish to avenge my father's downfall. He bet everything he owned on a game of cards. I want to restore the honor of his name back to my family."

"You play a dangerous game. Do you know who your father lost this card game to?"

"Yes."

"Then you are aware of the full scope of that game and the entirety of what your father lost."

"I know that he lost everything he owned that was not entailed."

Belle realized the girl was unaware she had been the end focus of the legendary card game. Her father gambled away something that wasn't his. However, it wasn't Belle's secret to tell. For Belle to come to a decision, she needed to know more of the lady's emotions.

"How do you plan to win back your father's wealth? Once you step foot in The Wager, you will be ruined. Not to mention the wrath of your brother and his peers would cause me to lose my business. You are asking me to risk everything I own for your silly card game. From what I hear, your brother is rebuilding your family's wealth with the funds from his wife."

"Is it silly to want to gain back my family's pride? Lord Holdenburg brought about our demise and pretends to be a friend of our family while we have suffered. That is not an act of friendship. No, I will not rest until he has suffered as I have. Then and only then will I feel that I have defended my father's honor," Kathleen passionately declared.

"Do you yourself not hold any feelings for Lord Holdenburg? No act of friendship?" Belle asked.

"None."

Kathleen's denial conflicted with memories of his kisses. She wouldn't discuss any more with the Madame for fear of betraying herself.

Belle watched the doubt cloud Lady Kathleen's eyes. There was a story there, one Belle wanted to learn more. However, with every good story one must allow the tale to unfold. Before this ended, much drama would occur. Along the way she hoped to guide it to a happy ending.

"Very well, I will take on your sponsorship. On one condition."

"At that may be?"

"At any time that I wish to know more details, you will provide them with honesty. If I feel you are being dishonest, I will revoke your membership. I understand the pain and suffering your family has endured. However, I feel that you lay fault with the wrong man. There was another man involved in your father and Holdenburg's card game. You are blaming a man who only tried to save your family."

"I agree to your terms, Madame Bellerose. But I hold a different opinion and will have to disagree on how you viewed the outcome of that game. I hold my own beliefs and those are the ones which drive me to my revenge. I appreciate your offer and I promise I will not risk your livelihood in the process."

"Please call me Belle."

"Belle."

"I insist that when you enter my establishment, you please wear a mask or a hood. In the card room, you must wear a mask at all times. I admire your brother and do not wish for him to have knowledge of my betrayal of our friendship. There is a small room I make available to the ladies of the ton for their discretion. I can lead you there now where you may choose a mask to wear. I assume you wish to play this evening?"

"Yes. Thank you for your generosity."

"Do not make me regret my decision, Lady Kathleen."

"Please refer to me as 'Scarlet' while I am here."

"Mmm … yes, a most befitting name for you."

Belle led Kathleen to the room where she made the choice to wear a mask of black silk. Red beads decorated the trim. The mask covered half her face, making her unrecognizable. It matched her dress perfectly. Once she finished hiding her identity, Belle escorted her to the entrance of The Wager. She then left Kathleen to her own devices.

Chapter Eight

Devon hunched over his countless drink of the evening. No matter how much he drank, Devon couldn't wipe away the taste of her luscious lips. Kathleen's sweetness invaded his soul and took root. If Devon spent the remainder of the night drinking endlessly, it still wouldn't be enough.

"I thought I might find you in here this evening."

"Enjoying your spirits, Belle," Devon slurred, lifting his glass in a toast.

Belle slid into a chair across from him. The frown on her face marred her perfect beauty. Why didn't he fall for Belle, who kept her emotions contained? Why did he fall for the one lady in London who wanted nothing to do with him?

"Belle, do you want to run far away from this dissolute, depraved city?"

"Where would we go, Devon?"

"Where we could lose ourselves in the pleasures of our passion."

"As tempting of an offer as that may be. I will have to decline. I would not satisfy what you hold dear in your heart."

"Nor what you hold dear in yours?"

Belle nodded.

"He is a fool."

"Who is a fool?"

"The man who stole your heart and keeps it prisoner, so you are unable to love another."

"My, you are deep in your cups this evening, my lord. You speak utter rubbish."

"No, I do not, my dear. But I will allow you your secrets, even though you refuse to allow me the same discretion."

"I interfere because I wish for you to achieve happiness. Your guilt eats away at your soul bit by bit every day."

"I would need a soul for that to happen, Sweet Belle."

"Why the drink?"

"I am trying to wash away her sweetness."

"Whose?"

"My guilty conscience."

"Is it working?"

Holdenburg's harsh laugh gave Belle the answer. It would appear the earl had begun his pursuit of the lovely lady. How would Holdenburg react when he heard the very lady has now entered the gaming hell? Belle had to handle this with a tactic to make the earl realize the girl would be safe. If there were ever two people who needed brought together, it was these two. Along the course of the way Belle would need to guide Holdenburg on how to win the lady's hand, and highlight to Lady Kathleen the gentleman by showcasing Holdenburg's character.

Belle slid the tokens across the table, placing them in front of Holdenburg's glass. He glanced at them for a second, then poured himself another drink. Once he tossed the fiery liquid back, he flipped the coins back and forth, over and over. Belle waited for his reaction, but like the ultimate card player, he never gave himself away. Holdenburg arched his eyebrow in question.

She said, "Those had belonged to—"

"I know who the owners of these tokens are. Why are you in possession of them?"

"On two different occasions, they were presented to Ned. A few weeks ago, a young boy knocked on the door and tried to gain entrance with the green token."

"And the red coin?"

"This evening a lovely lady in a dark red gown tried to enter with it. She had long, black raven hair and called herself Scarlet. A fitting name, for her attire matched her to perfection."

"Scarlet?"

"Mmm. Yes, that is the name she provided. When I denied her access, she told me a story that touched at my heart. We reached an agreement after she agreed to my conditions. I offered her my sponsorship to the club. Full access. But she only wanted the gaming hell. I think perhaps the brothel tempted her, but she was too much of a lady to ask questions."

"What in the hell have you done?"

Holdenburg watched Belle relax in the chair, confidence written all over her demeanor. Wave after wave of emotions flooded Devon. Kathleen had gained access to The Wager. Only one reason would prompt this madness. Kathleen came for revenge. Devon's hope to draw her into a courtship was futile at this point.

Devon's first reaction was to drag Kathleen kicking and screaming from The Wager. Then there was his devious side that wanted to play her game. She obviously wore one of the many masks Belle provided the ladies who wished to indulge in scandalous pursuits. Kathleen's identity would stay hidden. Perhaps, with his inside knowledge, Devon's pursuit of Kathleen Beckwith would be more exciting. He understood her well enough to know she would find any means to seek revenge and would keep returning. So why not use this to his advantage? Devon could court Kathleen with their mother's pressure upon her and win her over. Or tempt her with a passion she would find hard to deny. If Devon played ignorance of her identity, then he could protect her better. She played a dangerous game though, because Lord Velden still wished to win her. With Belle's assistance he could keep Kathleen's identity a secret from Lord Velden. If the lord had any inkling Kathleen was in attendance, he would set about her ruination with a pleasure the vindictive man craved.

"From the emotions crossing your face, you reached the same conclusion I did."

"We cannot stop her?"

"No, I am afraid not."

"Then we must let her achieve the goal she seeks as soon as possible."

"Even when her goal is your demise?"

"Yes."

"How do you wish to proceed, my lord?"

"I assume her identity is kept a secret?"

"She wears a mask as we speak. I will have Ned and a couple of extra guards stay near her at all times unless you are with her."

"Scarlet?"

"Yes, she wishes to go by the name of Scarlet."

Devon smiled at the choice of name. The clever minx, but not clever enough. She gave herself away with that name. Devon was well aware of the name of Kathleen's favorite theater actress. Scarlet Nightengale.

"I will play along with her devious game. However, do not tell her I know 'tis her. I do not want to draw any more attention to her than necessary. Only this very evening Lord Velden goaded me to play another hand to win her. He will stop at nothing until he has her. I will not give him any more ammunition."

"I cannot deny him access. He has broken no rules to my establishment, therefore I do not have cause to forbid him entry."

"I understand, Belle, and I do not expect you to play favors. I only beg for your assistance in helping me keep Lady Kathleen out of his grasp."

"Whatever you may need, I am at your disposal. The urgency to keep this a secret is just as strong for me. If Rory were to get wind of this, I would not be able to recover from his wrath. Even with Sheffield and Wildeburg's support, there would be no survival from the repercussions."

Devon covered his hands over the coins and moved them into his pocket.

"I will make sure to return them to their rightful owners. We are in agreement then."

"Excellent. I will leave you to your drink. Good evening, Lord Holdenburg." Belle's voice rose, letting the other customers know they only enjoyed a friendly conversation.

"I believe I am finished here. Please, have your servant bring the bottle to the tables. I feel a streak of luck in cards."

Belle motioned for the barkeep to follow Holdenburg with his bottle of spirits. She then walked around to each table, making sure her customers were being taken care of. Belle made an offer to each man for time above stairs if any were interested. Belle needed to distract their thoughts from any curiosity they might hold for the lengthy conversation with Holdenburg. Once the gentlemen took Belle's offer, she returned to the office to contemplate her decision. Belle only hoped she hadn't made the biggest mistake of her life.

Chapter Nine

Devon strolled with a drunken stagger into the card room. Too most in the room he went unnoticed, his behavior the norm. Most evenings Devon was drunk into his cups beyond what most hoped to take advantage of. He always disappointed them. Even stinking drunk, barely holding himself up, Devon bested them. So tonight would be no different.

Devon searched the room. Most of the tables were full, making it hard for him to find Kathleen. However, it didn't take long to locate her. The seductive huskiness of Kathleen's laugh surrounded him when his eyes zeroed in on the divine creature surrounded by every reprobate of London. What in the hell was her body draped in? He scowled, advancing on her. Devon shrugged off his suit coat to cover her shoulders. Her breasts grabbed the men's attention with every set of eyes at the table drawn to the open display. The creamy white skin even beckoned Devon until he stood over her. When Devon looked down, he saw the valley between the bountiful globes pushed forward. The beading of her gown barely covered Kathleen's nipples. His cock hardened at the sight.

Devon's first instinct of dragging her from here almost took over. He resisted, because if Devon hauled Kathleen out, it would only be to take her upstairs into one of the bedrooms made available to him. There, he would strip her from the gown and take her with all the passion he had built up.

Kathleen would be no safer with him than with any of these other scoundrels. The temptation beckoned—of bending Kathleen's head back and plundering her lips while everybody watched.

When Kathleen glanced his way, Devon moved closer. She arched her brow, and he almost gave into his temptation again. Devon's drunken leer must have bothered her enough, because she shifted in her seat, trying to move away. He laughed to himself. Kathleen wasn't as confident as she tried to portray. Scarlet, indeed. Holdenburg plopped into the seat next to her, draping his coat over the back of the chair. This caused her to move farther away. However, this wouldn't deter Devon. The servant set the bottle of whiskey to his left. He lifted the bottle and took a swig.

He heard his name muttered in disgust by the other players. A couple even rose and left the table after paying Scarlet compliments to her card game. Then there were the others who tried to engage Devon in conversation. Some even tried to slander him with drunken names. Devon ignored every single one of them, keeping his gaze fastened on Kathleen. God, she was a beauty. Her maiden dresses never did her justice. Dark bold colors drew out her spirit. Still, Devon would love to see Kathleen in a dark sapphire dress, one much like this, for his viewing pleasure only. To keep his hands to himself would be a testament to his patience. But did he have to? Perhaps Devon could tempt Kathleen into more.

Kathleen stilled when Holdenburg slid into the chair next to her. The desire she saw in his eyes frightened her. When Holdenburg continued to regard her with the same intense stare, Kathleen trembled. Had she given herself away? Did Belle betray her confidence? Holdenburg reached out and slid a finger across her gloved hand. The touch seared Kathleen through the fabric. She yanked her hand away.

"Sir, you are taking liberties I have not allowed for you to take."

"Forgive me, my lady."

Kathleen didn't answer. She stacked her chips in front of her. Should she leave? Kathleen only wanted to test the waters this evening to see if she could fool others with her disguise. She'd learned how men who presented themselves as gentlemen in the ballroom took on a different behavior in a gaming salon. Their words were cruder, their attentions grabbier. Since Kathleen had been raised in a sheltered environment, their behavior caught her off guard. After she overcame her shock, Kathleen turned on her inner actress and pretended that her time in the gaming hell was a play. A play where she was the main star. Kathleen lied to herself though—a small part was vanity. Kathleen enjoyed the attention these men paid her, for some of them never gave her notice in a ballroom.

"Lord Holdenburg, may I take your suit coat?"

A scantily dressed lady called Eve approached Devon, slipping onto his lap. She stroked her hand across his chest, whispering in his ear on how she would keep it in her room, and he could collect it after he finished playing cards. The chit whispered loud enough for Kathleen to overhear. Devon watched Kathleen's body stiffen even more than it had from when he arrived at the table.

"What a kind offer, love. I shall see you soon. Now take yourself away, I have a lucky streak twitching in my fingers. If I win, it will be a pleasurable evening. If not, I shall let you console me later."

Eve slid off his lap after placing a kiss on his lips. She grabbed his coat, shooting a smirk in Kathleen's direction.

Kathleen returned Eve's smirk with a glare. Kathleen's fingers tightened on her chips, digging them into her hand. Why should Kathleen care how

Holdenburg spent the rest of his evening? He could bed every chit in this brothel with her permission, as long as he left her alone.

With his declaration of feeling lucky, the remaining players left the table. This left him alone with Kathleen. Devon had noted the signs of Kathleen's jealousy during his interaction with Eve.

"It would appear 'tis only you and me. What is your pleasure?" Devon drawled close to Kathleen's ear.

Kathleen knocked the stack of chips over at the whisper of Devon's breath across her neck. Devon's question of her pleasures flustered what remaining nerve she held. Kathleen felt the warm blush spreading across her cheeks. She tried restacking the chips but only caused the other pile to fall. Devon settled his hand over her shaking fingers.

"Allow me."

Kathleen pulled her hand out from beneath his, laying it in her lap, while Devon restacked her chips. Devon waved for an attendant to help them. With directions on cashing in her chips, they waited while the counter returned with the cash.

"Can I entice you into a game, my lady?"

"No, I must leave."

"Perhaps another time?"

"Perhaps."

Kathleen needed to leave now. She had ridden a high while winning a few hands of cards. But once Holdenburg sat at the table, all her confidence fled. Her nerves were on edge, afraid Devon would guess her identity. Even though he had yet to call her bluff, Kathleen still feared that he knew.

"Can I convince you to share a drink?"

"I must return home."

"Why?"

"Why what?"

"Why must you return home? The night is still young. There is much more to live."

"My husband will return soon."

"Your husband?"

"Yes, my husband. I need to be in bed before he arrives."

"May I ask where your husband may be?"

"Where the majority of husbands are at this time of night."

"And where may that be?"

"With their mistresses." Kathleen bit this out.

Kathleen wasn't a fool and knew where the gentlemen of the ton spent their evenings. She heard the rumors. A few months ago, Kathleen discovered her father indulged with many mistresses throughout his married life. Her brother and his friends were the few rare gentlemen who did not. But each of them were newly married. In time, who knows, even they might stray. Kathleen prayed not, but a man's mind was a complicated puzzle she had yet to understand.

"Your husband is a fool. 'Tis a shame to abandon one so lovely as you. If you need company to keep you warm in your bed before he returns, I would be more than happy to oblige."

"Ah, another man whose loyalty sways with his urges."

"But I am only a bachelor, I have no commitments to lay my loyalty with."

"Do you not owe loyalty to the lady who just shared your lap only moments ago? One who you pledged to visit later?"

"I made no promises to share her bed."

"But you more than implied you would."

"It is not but a matter on how she perceived it."

"Believe me, my lord. From my viewpoint and hers, she perceived you would."

"I beg to differ. Now, let us return to my offer."

"Which offer was that? The card game, the drink, or the offer to warm my bed?"

"All three, if you are lucky."

Holdenburg leaned back in his chair. He always enjoyed these little squabbles with Kathleen. Their play on words held for many enlightening conversations. This one even more so, since they pretended they didn't know one another.

Kathleen had to laugh. When Holdenburg unleashed his full onslaught of charm, he was hard to resist. But resist she must.

"Good evening to you, my lord." Kathleen rose.

"You may call me Devon. At Belle's we are an informal bunch."

"Devon."

"And what may I call you. I have many names I wish to whisper, but I will save those for a more intimate occasion."

"The only name you may call me is Scarlet. For I will never give you cause to call me by any other."

"I do love a good wager."

Kathleen rolled her eyes at his audacity. She set out to leave, but Devon kept following her. When Kathleen reached the darkened hallway leading to the exit, Devon pulled her into the shadows.

"I bet within the month, you will beg me to warm your bed and to whisper every name held in anticipation from my lips."

Before letting Kathleen go, Devon wanted one more sample from her sweet lips. He pulled Kathleen into his arms and kissed her deeply, leaving Kathleen no room to doubt his true intentions. When Kathleen moaned against him and wrapped her arms around his neck, Devon's kiss deepened.

"Devon, is that you?"

Eve was calling out. Kathleen pulled herself from his arms before she made any more of a fool of herself. Kathleen tasted the whiskey from his lips that wasn't there earlier in the evening. She closed her eyes for a moment before opening them to find Eve standing on the bottom step. She was wearing nothing but Devon's suit coat. Kathleen guessed that what they whispered about Devon Holdenburg held true. He was nothing but a womanizing, drunken gambler.

"Do not let me keep you, *Devon*." Kathleen purred his name the same way Eve did.

"But …"

"But what, my lord? You think because we shared an intimate moment there would be more to this evening?" Kathleen laughed, putting on her best performance of the evening. "While you kiss with a passion I have not experienced in a while, I am not looking for anybody to warm my bed. And if I so choose, I would be a lot more selective than somebody who stuck their prick into whoever turned their fancy at the moment."

Kathleen walked gracefully out of the shadows. Ned held the door open and helped her into a hackney. With the door standing wide open, Devon watched Kathleen turn and stare at him. Her bruising set down caused him to react in the stupidest of ways.

Devon walked over to Eve, spread open his coat, and wrapped his arms around the girl, pulling her in for a kiss. A kiss Devon should never had done. The kiss filled him with disgust of the worst kind. He lifted Eve in his arms and carried her upstairs. Once he reached the top landing he turned around for Kathleen's reaction. Any reaction to show she cared. However, he would be disappointed. Kathleen had left.

Chapter Ten

"Will your friend be able come to our assistance in uniting Devon and Kathleen?" Dallis asked.

Sophia and Sidney assured Dallis that she would. They shared a look of guilt at bringing Dallis here under her tender condition, but there was no other way. Belle didn't venture into society, and if Rory got wind of their whereabouts, he would be furious. They only hoped Dallis was as open-minded as they thought. If not, their plan was doomed.

"Your friend has excellent taste. Her home is most elegant."

"Um, Dallis, about that. Our friend is not your normal type of friend you might socialize with. She is ..." Sidney tried to describe Belle but didn't have the right words to explain how dear Belle's friendship was to them.

So Sophia attempted. "While Belle is a most extraordinary woman, we met under excruciating circumstances. However, we trust her, for she has been instrumental in the courtship of our marital unions."

"Belle? Belle, as in the same lady who employed Rory to fight? Belle, as in the owner of a brothel?" Dallis squeaked.

Sidney and Sophia winced. They waited for Dallis's angry reaction. Instead a devious smile spread across her face. With glances at each other in surprise, they relaxed.

"Oh, there is never a dull moment with you ladies. I am so glad to call you friends. Am I sitting in the brothel now?"

"Yes," answered Sophia.

"Is this where you and Alex ...?" Dallis twirled her fingers in the air.

Sophia blushed and nodded. The memories she shared with Alex in the room above stairs still brought about many scandalous thoughts. She wondered if she could convince Alex to return. Perhaps on their anniversary. Sophia brought herself back to the current conversation.

"I do not know what to say."

"Are you mad at us for bringing you here?" asked Sophia.

"No, I am delighted. Rory has not let me have any fun since I announced my pregnancy."

"Will you please keep knowledge of this visit from him and from our husbands? While Sheffield and Wilde encourage our friendship with Belle, they do not wish for us to be involved in any matchmaking schemes," Sidney explained.

"This will be our little secret. Rory is none too thrilled with Holdenburg and would be very angry if he knew that I conspired to push Kathleen into Holdenburg's open arms. I have not discussed with him the reason for his hostility towards Holdenburg, but I think it revolves around a bet made between his father and Holdenburg. After the ball last evening, I meant to discuss this with him, but I had to fake another illness to cover for Kathleen."

"Why did you need to cover for Lady Kathleen?" a voice asked from the door.

Dallis shifted in her seat to see the newcomer. An attractive woman walked in and sat across from her. This had to be Belle. Or was it? This wasn't a Madame, but a woman who held the appearance of a lady in society. She wore an elegant day dress of forest green. While not demure, it was still modest. The lady wore her hair in a bun, and a simple chain adorned her neck. She sat with a grace not expected of a Madame. However, after Dallis's foray into the ton, she learned most people were not who they appeared to be. And Belle, even though she was a Madame, had eyes which spoke of a sadness that pulled at Dallis's heart strings. This woman held her own story of heartache, and while the other ladies in the room enjoyed a happy ending to their stories, Belle did not. Dallis smiled at Belle, liking her at once. She understood why Sidney and Sophia cared for this woman. And if she was not mistaken, so did their husbands.

Belle relaxed. She had been nervous when her friends requested a visit and asked to bring Rory's wife, Dallis. Would this lady welcome a friendship? Belle feared she wouldn't. However, the smile the red head beauty bestowed on her spoke otherwise.

Dallis said, "I believe Lord Holdenburg kissed Kathleen. We could not find Kathleen for a spell. Lord Holdenburg had made note of her absence, discreetly of course. We separated to search for her, and I found her walking out from behind some dark columns. She held a faraway expression and muttered something about a kiss. Before I could inquire further, Mama and Rory joined us and Kathleen spun a story on her whereabouts. When I awoke this morning, Kathleen had already left with Mama."

"Do you think they shared a kiss?" Sidney asked.

Sophia shook her head at Sidney's dreamy voice. For someone who was once so cynical about love and romance, Sidney sure changed her opinion. Now, Sidney imagined there was a true love story for every couple.

"If not at the Camville Ball, then later in the evening, Holdenburg kissed Lady Kathleen. I witnessed it myself," Belle replied.

All three women swung their eyes toward Belle with their mouths hanging open in astonishment. Belle would have laughed at the comedy if she didn't need their help so badly. She worried she wouldn't be able to fulfill the promises she made to Lady Kathleen and Holdenburg.

"Do spill. This story keeps getting more scandalous by the minute," Sophia said.

Belle went on to explain what transpired at her establishment the previous evening. She told them everything, except for the details of the late Lord Beckwith's bet. Only a handful of people knew, and they swore Belle to secrecy. Belle even thought Dallis held no knowledge. Rory still hadn't confided everything to his wife. The fool. Did Rory not learn his lessons about keeping secrets? Belle finished with the kiss she'd observed when she followed Kathleen to the door. Belle told the ladies she wanted to make sure Kathleen left safely. When she finished the story with Holdenburg's idiotic display of anger with Eve, all three ladies' expressions changed from dreamy to fury.

"I assumed he cared for Kathleen. Maybe we are wrong to pursue this? If Holdenburg is to be so callous in sharing the sport of sex with multiple women, then we need to keep him from Kathleen," Dallis stated.

Sophia and Sidney murmured their agreement. Apparently, they had been wrong. Dallis had been positive Holdenburg loved Kathleen, falling for his charm in this matter. Holdenburg fooled her as he fooled everybody. Dallis felt ashamed for allowing him to be her friend.

Belle said, "You were not wrong in your assumptions of his feelings. However, you are wrong on his sexual pursuits."

"But he kissed Eve in front of Kathleen and carried her above stairs. His actions speak for themselves," Dallis argued.

"Yes, to most they would."

"Belle?"

"Yes, Sidney."

"What are you leaving out of your story?"

"Oh, I did not tell you he retrieved his coat from Eve and left shortly thereafter?"

Sophia laughed. "No, you left out the most important part of the story."

Dallis sighed with relief. "He loves her."

The ladies discussed how they would bring Devon and Kathleen together. Sophia offered to throw a dinner party in Dallis and Rory's honor in congratulations for the new baby. Sophia would invite Holdenburg and his parents. Belle would throw them together at every opportunity at her club. Dallis would encourage Devon to court Kathleen and win her heart the old-fashioned way. Every lady had a plan except for Sidney, who was the true matchmaker of the group. It was then they decided they would need to distract Rory. To accomplish this, Sidney would seek Rory's help with a scientific project. Her father came into some artifacts which needed cataloging. Sidney would keep Rory occupied with this while everybody else brought the couple together.

On their way out, Belle spoke to Dallis privately.

"Please accept my congratulations on your upcoming birth, Lady Dallis."

"Thank you, Belle. Please call me Dallis, we are now friends." Dallis reached out and squeezed Belle's hands in an act of camaraderie.

"Thank you, Dallis, for accepting me so openly."

"I want you to know that when the day comes and you want to unburden your sorrows, it would be my honor to have you confide in me."

Belle became choked with emotion at Dallis's offer. She always thought she hid her feelings away, but her new friend sensed her unhappiness. Belle nodded and Dallis gifted her with the same friendly smile and hugged her before leaving.

This last year had held many surprises for Belle. Welcome ones, but surprises, nonetheless. For years, her only true friends were Sheffield and Wildeburg. Sheffield helped during the worst time in her life. Their wives had opened their arms wide to offer Belle a woman's companionship that she only ever dreamed of. Now her circle of friendship had spread even wider with Rory and Dallis. Only one person would complete this circle, but he would be forever out of her reach.

Chapter Eleven

Kathleen sat in the overcrowded parlor, watching Holdenburg charm the variety of dim-witted girls who flocked here with their mamas to visit Holdenburg's mother. Since the duchess had returned to town, it gave them the excuse they needed to throw their daughters at the earl. Holdenburg enjoyed every moment, with every charming smile he would pay compliments to their dresses, and show sincere interest in what they spoke. Holdenburg gained the title of the most sought-after bachelor of the ton with these tactics. Even with his title of scoundrel, it still didn't deter their pursuit. For he was also wealthy in his own right. His father held a dukedom, and Holdenburg would inherit with many family holdings, however Holdenburg had already gained his own fortunes from gambling. He had been the demise of many family's ruin. Nonetheless, they still clamored for his attention. The mamas hoped for him to ruin their daughters with his scandalous ways. They urged their daughters to trap him in whatever way possible. Holdenburg always managed to escape from their clutches. While he ruined many of them, their parents never caught him in the act. The whispered sighs in the back of the ballrooms were proof of his rakish behavior.

The duchess told Kathleen, "I am sorry, my dear, for this mad rush. Soon, these fools will leave and we will have time for our discussion."

"I understand."

"I do not comprehend why they deemed my parlor the destination for calls today."

"It is because of your presence in town. They now have an excuse to throw their daughters at Holdenburg."

"A waste of time on their parts."

"I think differently. He finds pleasure in their company."

"Then you are as much of a fool as they are, my dear."

"Excuse me, Your Grace?"

"You heard me."

"Yes, I did. But I do not understand."

"My son only has eyes for one lady."

Kathleen looked over at Holdenburg to see who had taken hold of his attention. Her eyes clashed with his. Holdenburg looked directly at Kathleen. When he wouldn't break eye-contact, Kathleen turned away. The duchess patted Kathleen's hands in understanding.

"You must realize it is our greatest wish, your mother and I, for you and Devon to make a union."

"'Tis not possible."

"Why not?"

"Because your son and I can barely tolerate each other. We would kill each other before the honeymoon even finished."

The duchess laughed. Yes, Kathleen was perfect for her son. She loved Kathleen as a daughter. When Devon and Rory ran as boys, they always left Kathleen alone where she spent time with the ladies. The duchess passed her love of the theater onto the girl, and they enjoyed many passionate discussions of plays and the actors and actresses. She felt Devon harbored feelings for Kathleen and had yet to pursue them. But she'd noticed a change in her son since their return to the city. Devon carried himself with a tension she had never seen before, especially around Kathleen. And if the way Devon regarded the girl this afternoon was any indication, then he meant to pursue Kathleen. Yes, they would make beautiful babies. She wanted to discuss with Lady Beckwith how to bring them together.

The duchess didn't reply to Kathleen; instead she walked away with a wink. Soon the parlor emptied when it became time for the fashionable hour to end. When Kathleen and her mother remained sitting, the other mamas and simpering chits shot glares in their direction. The Duchess of Norbrooke, with her charming nature, promised to invite them for a luncheon party soon. The invitation appeased the ladies, offering another chance to pursue Holdenburg again.

"Finally, what a madhouse this afternoon," the duchess said.

Holdenburg laughed. "You are the one at fault, Mother. This was never an issue while you and Father were at your country estate."

"I am at fault? No, my son. I am only the excuse they used to call. You alone lay in fault. They came to shove their daughters under your nose to make a choice."

"Then they are all fools. None of those chits meet my standards. I have already made my decision and when I am ready, I will let it be known. In the meantime, I do enjoy the extra attention."

Both of the older ladies laughed. However, a sense of loss settled over Kathleen. While Kathleen didn't want Holdenburg for herself, she didn't want him for anybody else. Once he married, they would no longer spar. It wouldn't be appropriate, nor would his bride allow it. When Holdenburg mentioned he'd already made a choice, her heart stopped. She could no longer deny what he meant to her. Holdenburg meant more to Kathleen than she wanted to admit. It was so much easier to deny the emotion. Kathleen would have thought, after she witnessed him carry the harlot up the stairs after their passionate kiss, it would have destroyed any small amount of affection she held. Kathleen returned home where she laid in bed, suffering an ache she didn't understand. Tears had streamed down her face as she imagined him making love to the beautiful blonde. Why did he kiss her so passionately one moment and then bed another so easily? But he didn't kiss her, did he? He kissed Scarlet. He propositioned Scarlet. Not Kathleen. She'd confused herself with her own deception. Was she in over her head?

Devon said, "If you ladies will excuse me, I promised Father a discussion on the estate."

"Of course, dear. Kathleen and I can gossip on the new play hitting the theater this week."

"I have already extended them an invitation for opening night."

"Excellent, you think of everything, Devon."

"Enjoy your talk and I will visit with you ladies at a later time."

When Devon left, Kathleen felt rejected. Not once through the afternoon did he even acknowledge her, unless you count the stare he regarded her with. She'd expected something from him after the kiss at the Camville Ball. But Devon Holdenburg had disappointed Kathleen yet again.

Soon the duchess and Kathleen held a deep discussion on which actors would be in the play. Her Grace had gained access to watch a dress rehearsal and regaled Kathleen with the set designs and costumes. They laughed over the ridiculous decisions the writer demanded and awed over the choices in the actors for the play. The director had chosen her favorite actress, Scarlet Nightengale, for the lead. The duchess promised Kathleen an introduction on opening night. With her donations to the playhouse, they gave her access to the backstage.

When they finished their discussion, talk turned to their charity work. Kathleen excused herself with a request to walk in the gardens. Opening the French doors, Kathleen strolled outside into the beautiful day. The full blooms beckoned to help calm her soul. Kathleen walked along the gravel path, bending to smell the flowers when she came upon them. Following the walkway, she located a bench and sat upon it, lifting her face to the warmth of the sun. Kathleen relaxed, gathering her scattered emotions under control.

~~~~~~

Devon's distraction came into his sight. Once he saw Kathleen walk into the garden, he lost all track of his father's conversation. His father again lectured him on his need to secure a bride. Ever since Rory wed Lady Dallis MacPherson, his father became more demanding for Devon to settle. Once his father discovered Devon courted the lovely Dallis, but failed to secure her as a bride, Devon had endured many such lectures. Dallis carried a wealthy dowry that would have added to their fortune. Not that they needed money. They were as rich as Croesus. But to his father, their current finances were never enough. The duke wanted the family's wealth secure for generations to come. His father thought him a wastrel, believing the rumors of his gambling and whoring. Who was Devon to correct his father? His mother, on the other hand, knew of his true nature. Plus, she was a mother. Devon could do no wrong in the duchess's eyes.

However, the lady walking through the gardens thought everything he did was wrong. Devon had acted like a fool last night. What prompted him to behave in that nature still confused him. When Kathleen arrived today, she kept her distance, her gaze skittish, and the hurt in her eyes tore at his soul. Devon caused Kathleen's pain. However, he couldn't apologize, because then he would give away the knowledge that he knew it was her and not Scarlet.

"You could do worse. In fact, she is your mother and I's first choice. She would make a lovely addition to our family."

"You forget, Father, she would bring no coin to add to our coffers," Devon replied sarcastically.

The intention to antagonize his father failed. All he received was his father's laughter and a slap on the back.

"She would bring more than money to the table, my boy. But then I think you already realize that. You hold the same look I held for your mother when I courted her."

"Your eyesight is failing in your old age, Father. You speak rubbish."

"Do I?"

"Humph."

Devon ignored his father's amusement to return his attention on Kathleen. Devon wanted to join her, but he noticed a sense of calm settle over her and didn't want to interrupt Kathleen's peace of mind. His father continued to bait him, taunting him with Kathleen's beauty and keen sense of mind. If his father meant to bombard Devon with Kathleen's many amazing attributes, then he might as well step into the garden and disturb her.

Devon slipped out the door and walked along the grass pathway leading to the bench. He didn't want to scare Kathleen away before he even had the chance to approach her. Kathleen's head tilted back, the sun bathing her beauty. When Devon stood above her, he cast a shadow. Kathleen pierced him with a look, leaving him speechless and humbled to be in her presence. She smiled at him, the kind of smile which the other chits from this afternoon gave him. Devon should be wary of her sudden change of attitude, but it was a beautiful sight. It lit her face with a grace only Kathleen could pull off. Then when her smile carried to the secretive twinkle in her eye that he always wondered about, Devon caught his breath. Kathleen only ever gifted those close to her with *this* smile. Devon should know, he envied the lucky bastards. Mostly her family, but still, Devon had always craved for Kathleen to bestow one on him, just once. Finally, she gave him one.

Kathleen decided, while she rested in the garden, to come to terms with the emotions Devon stirred in her soul. If she explored her feelings with him as Kathleen and Scarlet, she could gain knowledge to his true character. After talking with his mother today, she reached an understanding that their families wished for them to marry. If Kathleen were to object, then she would draw attention her way. But if Kathleen were to encourage Devon's courtship, then she could destroy him as Scarlet. Either way, she would make him suffer. What better solution than to make her own terms than to have her mother's agenda forced onto Kathleen. Her family was unaware of a secret that the duchess kept as her own secret. Kathleen had private acting lessons when she was younger. She would take those lessons and apply them to her life. Kathleen would fool everybody into thinking she accepted Devon's courtship.

Kathleen slid over on the bench and patted the space next to her. She dazzled Devon with the smile she used on her family to gain her way. When Devon returned her smile with one of relief, Kathleen knew he fell for her tactics.

"Your mother has a beautiful garden."

Devon laughed. "You know my mother has no interest in flowers. Her only love is the theater. My father is the one who toils with the garden's beauty."

"His Grace?"

"Yes, but it is a highly kept secret. Your very life is now in danger with your knowledge of this information," Devon whispered.

This was the Devon she fell in love with all those years ago when she was a young girl. The one who was playful and kind. The one who used to convince Rory not to torment her.

"I will not tell a soul." She pretended to turn a key on her lips and toss it behind her.

Devon grabbed her hand before she tossed the pretend key away and continued to play by slipping it from her fingers and sliding it inside his suit coat.

"For safekeeping."

"Yes, of course."

Devon laid Kathleen's hand back on her lap, not taking any liberties as he did the night before. Kathleen rubbed her hand across the one he'd held for a brief pause. His heat invaded the thin material.

They sat in silence, neither one of them knowing what to say. Devon didn't want to anger Kathleen with any more of his arrogance, nor did he want to show his interest in case she didn't share the same. They watched the butterflies flitting around the garden as contentment settled around them. Devon's actions had caused many blunders, and he would repair them on the morrow. For now he would enjoy her company, as quiet as it may be.

When her mother beckoned for them to leave, Kathleen rose and turned to him, offering a small curtsey.

"Thank you for your lovely company, my lord."

"It was my pleasure, my lady."

With that, Kathleen left, leaving them with a sense of starting over. Perhaps, over time, she would allow him to display his true feelings. If she didn't, he would be a lost soul forever at her command.

Chapter Twelve

Kathleen once more donned the red creation she kept hidden under her bed. She risked getting caught, sneaking out two nights in a row, but the need to be near Devon after their peaceful afternoon held too much of a temptation.

Kathleen spent the evening enjoying a quiet family dinner with Rory doting on Dallis as usual. No one uttered the name Devon Holdenburg. Her mother and Dallis knew, if they mentioned the gentleman's name, it would send her brother on a tirade nobody wanted to endure. So their conversation consisted of the play they were to attend next week and the baby. Kathleen and her mother were just as excited as Rory and Dallis. It was a new beginning for their family. One that would bring much joy. When Rory and Dallis retired to bed early, her mother pleaded for Kathleen to excuse her too. Mama wished to retire early after their long afternoon. Kathleen assured her mother she would be reading a book to finish the evening.

Once the house quieted, Kathleen walked the same path outside to the hackney waiting in the alleyway. Kathleen had caught their gardener stealing vegetables to take home to his family, and then bribed the man with a promise not to tell Rory. All he must do was to have a hackney waiting when she requested. If he continued to do her bidding, she would keep his secret. Not that Rory would have fired the man, but the gardener didn't know this. He was a new servant and didn't know of her family's giving nature. Kathleen should feel ashamed of her deception, but she had a game to play and couldn't afford to show kindness right now.

When she arrived at The Wager, the door was opened by the man Belle referred to as Ned, greeting her with acceptance. He ushered her to the private room. With a discreet knock, Belle entered before Kathleen could answer.

"Back to back nights, my lady?"

"The temptation of cards was too hard to resist," Kathleen answered.

"Cards or Lord Holdenburg?"

"They are one and the same, are they not?" Kathleen turned the Madame's question back onto her.

Belle nodded.

Kathleen's fingers trailed across the gowns hidden in the wardrobe. They were made out of sheer material.

"Those are at your disposal too, along with the masks. If you ever want to entertain a certain gentleman."

Kathleen didn't respond. Instead, she searched for a mask to wear. In her anger the evening before, she had thrown the mask out of the window on the carriage ride home.

"I fear I owe you a new mask. In my frustration, I discarded the other one."

Belle swiped her hand through the air, indicating it was of no bother. With an intuitive expression Belle kept regarding Kathleen. The lady read more into what Kathleen didn't say. Kathleen would need to hide her vulnerability better.

"I wanted to welcome you before you cleaned house. Many of the same gentleman from last night have inquired if you would join us this evening. I will have to enlighten them with the delightful news. Also, I wanted to tell you that after you left, Lord Holdenburg's actions with Eve were only—"

"I do not care how Lord Holdenburg seeks his pleasures." Kathleen cut Belle off.

"You are mistaken by what you saw."

"As I said, it makes no difference to me."

Belle sighed. She noticed the hurt in the girl's eyes. Kathleen was only trying to protect herself from hearing what she thought was of Holdenburg seeking comfort in another woman's arms. Even though he didn't. Belle wanted to relieve Kathleen's heartache, but the girl remained stubborn. Belle had tried. Now it would be up to Holdenburg to convince the girl otherwise.

"Very well. Enjoy your evening, my lady. When you are ready, please allow Ned to assist in your return home."

Kathleen nodded. When Belle left, Kathleen realized she owed the lady an apology for her rudeness. But she couldn't handle hearing anything about Devon and that sensuous creature. Kathleen took a deep breath and remembered their time in the garden. Once Kathleen felt a sense of peace, she chose a mask and made her way to the card room.

The gentlemen she'd played with the previous evening called out their greetings, many offering a place at their tables. Holdenburg, who was involved in the middle of a game, took no notice. Kathleen was as invisible to him now as she was during tea this afternoon. She tried not to let it bruise her ego. Nonetheless it did, although he thought her to be Scarlet, not Kathleen. She would play his game of indifference. If Kathleen knew Holdenburg like she did, he would seek her out. Holdenburg could never deny a challenge. When another offer rang out to join a table, Kathleen took a seat.

All the gentlemen introduced themselves even though Kathleen already knew most of them. It amused her, all the same. The final gentleman at the table surprised Kathleen. The gentleman, who rescued her in the maze sat across from her. He pierced Kathleen with a gaze, taking in her attire. A devious grin lit his face as he welcomed her to their table. When he began the game and he paid no more attention to her than any other player at the table, Kathleen released a sigh of relief. Kathleen had fooled Lord Velden too.

Players came and left throughout the hands of cards played. Before long, Lord Velden, moved to the chair next to her. He whispered endearments as they played, causing Kathleen to blush as no married woman should. He was shameless, but tempting. Kathleen allowed his flirtations to stroke her ego after being ignored by Holdenburg—who still had yet to show any interest in her this evening. Kathleen laughed with the gentleman, causing many to look their way. After winning many hands, she declared a need to leave.

"Ah, my lady, this evening will pale without your presence. How am I to enjoy myself without your beauty?"

"I fear I must return before my husband arrives home."

He lifted her hand, sliding the glove off to see if she wore a wedding ring. While his touch sparked an interest, it didn't hold the same as when Holdenburg touched her. Out of the corner of her eye, Kathleen noticed she had finally gained Holdenburg's attention. She decided to play along with the lord's flirtation to see how Holdenburg would react.

"A shame, my lady, that your husband does not appreciate your fine beauty."

"His loss, your gain, my lord."

The lord placed a kiss on the knuckle above her ring. Abruptly, a chair was shoved against the wall and Holdenburg drunkenly plopped across from them, leering his disgust.

The gentleman ignored Holdenburg, but Kathleen struggled not to look his way. When the lord's fingers tightened on hers, her eyes went to their joined hands. Kathleen tried to pull away, but he held on.

"I think the lady wants her hand back, Lord Velden."

"I think you do not know what the lady desires. Sod off, Holdenburg, you are interrupting."

"I am only trying to prevent you from making an arse out of yourself as usual. But please proceed, I am enjoying the show."

Devon threw back another drink, controlling his temper. He wanted to reach across the table and trounce the bounder. Instead Devon relaxed, pretending an indifference he didn't hold. What bothered him more than anything was Kathleen appeared not to mind. It was as if she enjoyed Velden's attention. Which only made Devon drink more.

Kathleen said, "My lord, perhaps we can continue this discussion another evening? For now the hour grows late. If I am discovered, then I can no longer return."

Kathleen drew her hand out from Lord Velden's grasp. Once Devon joined their table, all the fun had gone at trying to make him jealous. The only act Kathleen managed was to enflame his temper. Kathleen heard Devon's menacing tone underlined by his threat. He might have shown an indifference to Lord Velden's attention, but Kathleen knew better.

Kathleen rose and pressed her fingers on the lord's shoulder. She bent over and whispered a promise of another time before she arched her eyebrow at Devon.

"Lord Holdenburg."

"Lady Scarlet."

Kathleen turned and quit the room. Devon sent a signal for Ned to follow her. He wanted more than anything to keep an eye on her, but he needed to stay at the table and taunt Lord Velden. If not, then the lord would have followed Kathleen and she would no longer remain safe.

Devon said, "It would appear another lady holds both of our interest."

"Yes, it would *appear* so, but she only holds interest in one of us. It would seem you have left the lady cold."

"A temporary setback. She will beg for me to bed her before the week is over," Holdenburg said.

"Shall we make a bet on the lovely Scarlet?"

"No, Lord Velden. I will no more bet on Lady Scarlet than I will bet on Lady Kathleen. No lady deserves your dishonor."

"However, you staked everything you owned on Lady Kathleen's honor a few years ago. Hell, you own the chit and she does not even realize it."

"Only to keep her out of your reach."

Lord Velden didn't answer Holdenburg. Instead, the lord gave him a smile, sending a shiver of warning down Holdenburg's back.

"Well, if you will not bet on who gets to enjoy the delectable Scarlet first, I shall have to make it my personal goal to best you."

Holdenburg tightened his grip around the glass. It was either that or he would wrap his fists around the lord's neck and squeeze until he left not a single breath in Velden's despicable body.

"You can try."

"I think before the season is through I will not only bed Lady Scarlet, but I shall also enjoy the delectable delights of Lady Kathleen. Once I have ruined her and walked away, you can try to win her hand. But before I release her from my clutches, I will spill your story. Then she will only look upon you with disgust. I will take great pleasure from your demise."

Once Lord Velden left the room, Holdenburg released a growl before hurling his glass at the wall. His built-up frustration raveled out of control. Holdenburg stalked from the room, hoping Kathleen hadn't left. When he saw Ned guarding a room on the lower level, he knew she remained. He dismissed Ned with a nod. The guard looked him over before he left. Ned would report his behavior to Belle. Holdenburg didn't care. Kathleen was under his protection, and nobody would keep him from her.

He threw the door open and found Kathleen still in her mask. She had one leg pulled up on the stool, adjusting her silk stocking. Holdenburg's eyes devoured Kathleen's long luscious legs that seemed to go on for miles. Every inch of them. If only Kathleen held her dress a little higher, he could see his greatest wish. Kathleen looked over her shoulder before she slowly slid her dress back down.

"Lord Holdenburg, to what do I owe this unexpected arrival?"

"I did not have time to enjoy your company this evening."

"Yes, well, I enjoyed the company of Lord Velden this evening instead. A most charming gentleman."

Kathleen baited Devon, watching the jealousy in his expression. He deserved a lot more grief, considering his actions from the night before. The only difference being was that she didn't kiss the lord or bed him the way

Devon did Eve. Devon's betrayal would always hold strong in Kathleen's heart.

"One rule in this establishment, my lady. Not everybody is who they portray themselves to be. Someone of Lord Velden's ilk uses his charming nature to draw in his prey before he eats them like the vulture he is."

"Nonetheless, I found him charming all the same. At least he focused his attention on me and not some random strumpet he only sought to use for his sexual urges."

Holdenburg advanced on Kathleen, standing but a breath away from her. He bent his head to kiss a trail along her neck.

"Have you never felt the need to give into your desires? To have your urges fulfilled. A lonely lady such as yourself, must have needs."

Kathleen couldn't breathe, let alone speak. Devon continued his onslaught of kisses down her neck and left a path of burning heat across her chest. His tongue now stroked alongside the beads across her breasts.

"I can fulfill those needs if you so desire. You have only to ask and I am yours."

Somehow he had loosened her buttons, and her breasts spilled out into his hands. Devon's thumbs brushed across her nipples, causing them to tighten into hardened buds. Kathleen heard his growl as he lowered his head to draw them into his mouth. He stroked her very desires. Kathleen wanted to beg him to make her his. Even though Devon had performed this very act with Eve the evening before, Kathleen no longer cared. Devon's passion set Kathleen's soul aflame.

"Scarlet," he moaned.

Kathleen tasted as sweet as he knew she would. Her body responded to his touch. He played her body with his desires. Devon bent her backwards, laying her upon the couch, and dropped to his knees. Devon glided Kathleen's gown up her legs, the very legs he had only just admired. Her silk stockings stopped mid-thigh, held with tiny clips. Devon unclipped them and the stockings slid off. Kathleen's white creamy thighs begged for his lips. His hand caressed the silken flesh, causing another moan to slip from his lips. When Devon pushed Kathleen's dress higher, the vision before him caught him off guard. Kathleen wore nothing underneath. Her dewy wetness beckoned him forward to sample the sweetness. Devon brushed across it and groaned. Kathleen was a temptation that laid before his eyes.

A temptation he couldn't resist. By all rights, Devon should ask her for permission, but he didn't. If she had been Kathleen, he would pay her the respect she deserved, but as Scarlet she understood the score. They were two consenting adults giving into their pleasures.

Devon lowered his head and slid his tongue across the beckoning dew. He savored her as she sunk into him. When Kathleen's fingers slid through his hair, he was lost. Devon pleasured Kathleen until she became undone at his touch. Her moans echoed around the room while he devoured her with each stroke. When Devon slid a finger inside her, Kathleen tightened around him. Kathleen's body pulsed with a need, and he wanted to help her release. His tongue flicked across her clit, stroking her to a higher level.

"Devon," she moaned.

Kathleen's body felt tightly strung. When Devon started his onslaught of seduction, she was powerless to stop him. His touch consumed her, his tongue devouring her. Kathleen ached for so much more. She watched his head lower to taste her. His hands gripping her thighs. The ache only grew the more Devon seduced her. Only Devon could help her. Kathleen's body ached for something she held no clue to. Devon's tongue drew out every sensation.

"Devon," she moaned as her body floated away.

When Kathleen moaned Devon's name, her body released the ache consuming her body. Devon drowned in her sweetness. His tongue stroked her quivers away. Devon moved his mouth to kiss the inside of her thighs. He softly stroked them as the tremors calmed. Devon slid up Kathleen's body. He gently nipped her buds and slid them inside his mouth for a gentle sucking. He continued to her lips, where he took her mouth in a kiss more passionate from when he began. Devon ached for her. He needed her so badly. He wanted to divulge Kathleen of the rest of her dress and slide his cock deep inside her wet heat. Devon wanted her fast and hard. Slow and soft. Anyway he could have her. Devon's need for Kathleen slipped out of his control.

He needed to leave now. If not, then he couldn't be held responsible for what he would do next.

Devon expected anger after her body calmed, but Kathleen returned his kiss with passion. Kathleen clung to Devon, her hands taking their own path on his body. This was madness. He pulled away, bringing her hands in between their bodies and holding them still. A cloud of confusion filled her eyes. Devon couldn't by all rights make love to her now.

Kathleen, in a daze of desire, couldn't understand why Devon stopped their lovemaking. He led them down a path that she wanted to follow. So why then did he stop?

"Lord Holdenburg?"

"Devon," he growled.

"Devon, are you putting a halt to our lovemaking?"

"No, my dear. I only paused so we could find a more comfortable place. I want to spend endless hours making love to you on a bed, not on a small couch in a dingy room."

Kathleen paused. If he were to make love to her, he would discover she was a virgin and not the married lady she professed to be. What had she done?

Kathleen pulled out of his arms and set her dress to rights. After she buttoned the dress and smoothed her hands down her skirts, she gifted him with a seductive smile.

"Would this be the same boudoir you used the night before? Does Belle keep a standing room available for you?"

Damn. He was doomed however he answered. While he pretended he didn't know who she was, Kathleen knew Devon. If he answered in the positive, it would calm Scarlet into believing he wanted no commitment. Where they could use the pleasure of each other's bodies to satisfy an urge. But if he answered in the negative, it would appear he wanted more. Devon wanted to give Kathleen the belief that he wasn't the scoundrel she thought him to be. Since no matter how Devon answered, the fates were not on his side, he decided to go with the truth.

"I used no room last night. Eve paled compared to your beauty. I only desired you. After I collected my coat, I made my way home. As for a standing room, Belle keeps one reserved for my use, if I so desire. Shall we?"

Holdenburg moved to the door and held it open, hoping Kathleen would follow him. When Kathleen gathered her reticule and shawl, walking in front of him, Holdenburg's knees weakened on her easy agreement. Holdenburg's greatest desire was about to come true.

However, before he could assist her up the stairs Kathleen requested a carriage from Ned. The guard stepped outside and hailed a hackney to take Kathleen home. She turned and bestowed Holdenburg with another smile. This one held something he had never seen before. Kathleen walked back to him and ran a finger down his chest. Her hand brushed across his hardness, her smile growing.

"Thank you, Lord Holdenburg, for satisfying a need my husband has been neglecting to fulfill."

With those words, Kathleen followed Ned outside and with his assistance entered the hackney. Holdenburg stood at the door, watching her drive away. He wore the look of a rejected lover. It would appear the chit had bested him again. Well, their next time, Holdenburg would satisfy his need with Kathleen begging for more. It was time to tease Kathleen with his attention, leaving her wondering. Holdenburg had charmed many ladies in his lifetime, but the charm he would unleash on Kathleen Beckwith would be like nothing she ever experienced before. Kathleen held no clue on what would come her way.

Chapter Thirteen

Kathleen awoke the next morning feeling more refreshed than she had in a long while. She laid in bed smiling, remembering the passion she shared with Devon. Kathleen should have been angry with him for taking advantage of her so shamelessly. But she couldn't, because Devon didn't take advantage of *her*. He shared an intimate moment with Scarlet. An experienced woman of the ton. One who knew how to enjoy the pleasures he provided. And my goodness, Devon knew how to pleasure a woman. His tongue stroking with a need only he could fulfill. What made the evening more of a success was Devon's confusion when she left. Kathleen's response dumbfounded him. Oh, the pleasure she felt from finally besting Lord Holdenburg. *Devon.*

Kathleen dressed and hurried downstairs. She had much to accomplish today. When she entered the dining room, it was to find her mother entertaining a guest. Not any guest, but Devon. He rose when Kathleen entered and waited until she sat before returning to his seat.

"Good morning, Mama. Lord Holdenburg."

"Good morning, dear."

"Good day, Lady Kathleen."

Kathleen poured tea and added sugar. She pulled the towel off the bowl and saw that Agnes, the cook, had made her favorite blueberry scones. Kathleen was famished this morning and loaded a plate with two scones.

Devon watched Kathleen add an obscene amount of sugar to the tea. She might as well have been drinking sugar water instead of ruining the good brew. Kathleen must have worked up an appetite. She was unabashed, eating with such gluttony in front of him. Kathleen moaned her delight when the blueberries burst on her tongue. Devon almost came undone. For it was the same moan she released when she burst upon his tongue. Devon shifted in his seat. Kathleen closed her eyes, moaning louder. Devon gulped.

"Kathleen, your manners."

"Sorry, Mama. But I am sure Lord Holdenburg knows the full delight of a special treat. Do you not, my lord?"

Kathleen wanted to laugh out loud at Devon's discomfort. She noticed him shifting in his seat when she moaned her delight.

Devon cleared his throat and gulped again. Kathleen gave him an innocent look, knowing Lady Beckwith thought Kathleen only asked an innocent question. The little minx. Well, two could play this game, my dear.

"Yes, I do, Lady Kathleen." He reached for a scone and broke it in two. Devon took a bite, groaning his own delight. "Mmm, yes delicious. Quite like a dessert I sampled last night. It was divine, and I savored every bite. I only hope I will be so lucky to sample it another time."

Kathleen's mother asked, "What was the dessert? Perhaps I can have Agnes make it for tea one day."

"Lord Holdenburg would have no knowledge of the ingredients, Mama." Kathleen tried not to choke on the scone at Devon's brashness.

"Your daughter is correct, my lady. I believe it to be a secret recipe. One only the owner can divulge under special circumstances."

"A shame then. You were lucky to enjoy the special treat."

"Very lucky indeed," Holdenburg replied, watching Kathleen for a reaction.

However, Kathleen held her card face, not showing her hand. The man was reprehensible. A devil, taunting with scandalous innuendos while in the company of her mother. Holdenburg knew no bounds.

"Can you wait while I retrieve the lists for your mother?"

Holdenburg stood when Lady Beckwith rose. "It would be my pleasure to spend a few moments in Lady Kathleen's company."

Kathleen waited for her mother to leave before she turned to Devon. When she glanced his way, she found him regarding her. He had a curious expression.

"Lady Kathleen, would you do me the honor of accompanying me on a ride in my phaeton this morning?"

"Yes, I would." Kathleen answered, surprising them both.

Devon sat nonplussed. He'd expected excuses, but Kathleen shocked him when she answered yes. Devon had hoped that she would accept—but that was all he had. Hope.

"Excellent."

Kathleen suspected he hadn't expected a yes. Kathleen found she wanted to spend time in Devon's company. Her curiosity got the better of her. Would he try to seduce her? He easily enough seduced Scarlet almost out of her dress the night before. But would he seduce Kathleen, the innocent debutante? How would Kathleen feel either way, if he tried to seduce or her not?

"I will gather my bonnet while you wait for Mama."

Devon rose when Kathleen left the table. He released the breath he had been holding. He walked to the window, running his fingers through his hair, realizing he was a fool when it came to Kathleen. What would she expect from their outing? Should he attempt to seduce her or court her properly? He didn't want her to believe that, as Kathleen, she was undesirable to him. She was anything but that.

Before Kathleen or Lady Beckwith returned, Dallis wandered into the dining room.

"Devon, what a joy. Would you like to join me for breakfast? I am a late riser this morning."

Devon assisted Dallis across the room and into a chair.

"I am sorry, I must decline. I have promised Kathleen a ride in my new phaeton. Also, Lady Beckwith is retrieving a list for Mama that I must deliver after my ride."

"Are you finally …"

"Yes."

Dallis squealed. "It is about time, my lord."

"Yes, a need to push this forward has come to light."

"I know."

"You do?" Holdenburg raised his eyebrows.

"Yes, Belle has confided in Sidney, Sophia, and myself."

"Damn her. She promised me this would go between nobody besides herself and me."

"Devon, you can trust us to keep this a secret."

"Does Rory know? Of course not, or I would not be left standing. How will you confess your involvement in this scheme to your husband? This will only bring forth problems in your marriage that I do not wish for you."

"No, he does not. I wish one of you would confide in me on the secret you hold. It has something to do with their father's final bet before he died. And the bet involved Kathleen. It does not take a fool to put two and two together to come to the conclusion on what I believe it may be."

"You are drawing fantasies where there are none."

"Devon, please allow me to help."

"No."

Before they could continue their conversation, Kathleen and her mother joined them.

Her mother told them, "Enjoy yourselves, children. I do not think Susan needs to chaperone. Devon is like family, practically a brother to you."

Kathleen and Devon offered their goodbyes as they headed along the sidewalk. Dallis and Lady Beckwith watched from the open doorway as Devon assisted Kathleen into a seat. He acted the perfect gentleman, seeing to her comfort. With a wave they were off. Both ladies sighed at the couple who made a perfect match.

"A brother to her?"

"Well, he is. They have known each other since they were children."

"Oh, Mama, you are a devious one."

"How do you imagine you and Rory came to be?"

"As, I said, devious."

~~~~~

Devon steered the horses along the road, taking the back roads to a surprise destination. He meant to take Kathleen to Hyde Park where everyone in the ton would see he courted her. Now Devon wanted to be alone with Kathleen. His selfish ways would be their demise. They were always in the company of others, his mother, her mother, Dallis, even Rory with his glare to keep his distance. How was Kathleen to take notice of his sincere acts of courtship if they were never left alone?

Kathleen wondered at their destination. Devon didn't make small-talk as they rode along. To be honest, the quiet companionship held a calming respite. Most of their conversations were threaded with sarcasm with each of them baiting the other. Even while she ate her breakfast, they sparred. Not in a cruel way, but still they sparred all the same. Kathleen relaxed, trusting him like she never had before. This past week he'd had perfect opportunities to ruin her name, but hadn't. Instead Devon sent her along on a passionate journey Kathleen hadn't expected. When Kathleen started with her plan, she had meant to ruin him. Now she only wished for Devon to ruin her. How ironic.

As the phaeton took them outside of the city limits and into the countryside, Kathleen sat forward, about to object to their destination. When he'd suggested a ride, she thought he would take them through Hyde Park. Kathleen feared Mama would worry at the length of time they were away. Why she feared that, who knows, her mama worshipped at Devon's feet. He could do no wrong in her mama's eyes.

Devon led them down a long drive to a lovely home nestled amongst a forest. Off to the side, Kathleen noted a pond within walking distance from the house. It was a two-story stately home, nothing so grand as what his family owned, but modest. English Oak trees lined the graveled drive with flowers welcoming them as they drove closer. It was quite lovely. She fell in love instantly and imagined young children running around the trees while she called out for them to be careful, with Devon looking on affectionately. Kathleen shook herself from the daydream, puzzled why the picturesque house drew her thoughts to that image. Kathleen wondered why Devon brought her here.

Devon brought the horses to a halt and assisted Kathleen down. A groomsman appeared out of nowhere and Devon offered him the reins and drew the man to the side with directions. Kathleen wandered away admiring the grand home. She turned toward Devon and waited for him. He appeared more relaxed when the servant cracked a joke, making Devon smile. He patted the groomsman on the back and turned toward her. Devon held out his hand and Kathleen walked to him, laying her palm in his.

Devon led Kathleen around to the rear of the house and gave her a tour of the grounds close to the house. He pointed out the path between the trees and explained about the structure of the house and when it was built. Devon spoke with pride when he described the house and grounds.

"This is yours?"

"Yes." He nodded, smiling around at his property.

"Why? When? How?"

"What question do you wish me to answer first?"

"All of them."

Devon laughed and began a tour of his home. When they reached what must have been his bedroom, Kathleen hovered inside the door. She took in the room decorated in different shades of blue. Kathleen's eyes lingered on the bed. The silk covers were a deep sapphire blue. What must be over twenty pillows of different shapes and sizes rested near the headboard. A more inviting sinful place there could not be.

"I would love to see you in a dark sapphire blue." Kathleen remembered Devon's comment.

Devon saw the pink blush spread across Kathleen cheeks when she stared at his bed. How would she look spread across his bed with the pink blush coloring her body? Devon had wondered this during many sleepless nights while lying in that empty bed. How he ached to discover now, but knew he shouldn't. It was too soon.

"As for your questions, my lady."

"Yes, my questions." Her eyes remained on the bed.

Did the same images flash across her mind as his? *Was it too soon?*

"As far as the how, what else am I supposed to do with my gambling winnings?" Devon laughed.

Kathleen stiffened. He dared to make a joke of stealing her family's worth.

Kathleen's demeanor quickly changed. His shallow comment offended her. Fool. Belle warned him that Kathleen believed he was the reason behind her father's demise.

"No, seriously. With a few shrewd investments, I was able to purchase this house."

"By the hands of other's ruin, you made those investments."

"No, Kathleen. I am wealthy in my own right. I only gamble because I find amusement in the games."

"Other people's unhappiness amuses you?"

"No, the pleasure of winning a hand of luck amuses me. I take no pleasure in another's demise. If a man is a fool to destroy his family with a hand of cards, then he deserves what he receives. It does not matter anyway. I pass my winnings in secret to their wives or children. I do not feel a family should suffer for the acts of their provider."

"But …" Kathleen paused. She couldn't mention her own father's foolishness without giving away her knowledge of that night. Did he not make the same offer to her family?

Devon knew what she wanted to ask. Yes, he tried to return Kathleen's father's money to Lady Beckwith, even the trump of the game. But Lady Beckwith had refused. Her pride kept her from accepting the kind offer. Devon thought the woman was even more devious than his own mother. While Lady Beckwith felt fury at her husband for betting on their own daughter's virtue as a stake in a card game, she was more than thrilled that Devon held the marker. Actually, she thought it was perfect. However, the guilt had eaten at Devon every day since that fateful night. His actions set about his own demise on winning the hand of Kathleen. Because once she discovered the truth, it would always leave a cloud of suspicion over their relationship.

"But what?"

"Nothing. Your actions are very noble, my lord."

There was nothing noble about him. If so, Devon would not have invited Kathleen inside his bedroom.

"And the when?"

"Three years ago."

His answer once again silenced Kathleen. The timeframe surrounded the death of her papa. The familiar ache overcame her at missing her beloved papa. A more loving father there could never be. She was aware of the scandal surrounding her father's death, even though Rory tried to shield her from it. And it tore at her mother's heart, racking her with unhappiness. However many faults her father may have held, he was still her father, and Kathleen loved him dearly. Never once in Kathleen's lifetime had her father not been her hero. Many would think that with the sins her father committed, he wouldn't be hero material. But her father loved Kathleen every day of her life and never gave Kathleen doubt of his love, and for that he would remain her hero.

"So, now that leaves the why."

"Many reasons."

"And they are?"

"I thought this would be a grand home for my wife. I pictured her here as we watched our children frolic in the open. It is close to the city and her family. Also, this place is my own. I adore my parents, but there are times I enjoy my own company."

"You knew your choice of bride three years ago?"

"Even before that, my dear."

Devon's tone had softened. When Kathleen looked into his eyes, his gaze scared her. The emotions revealed a look of love. He wasn't talking about her, was he?

Impossible.

Kathleen came further into the room, putting much-needed distance between them.

"Then why have you not pursued your choice of bride?"

When she turned around, Kathleen found Devon right behind her. He lifted his hand and brushed away a curl that had fallen loose. His touch gentle, so as not to scare her away.

"I never thought I stood a chance. She has only ever regarded me with disdain. It has only been recently that she has warmed to my presence."

"How recently?" Kathleen whispered.

"Today, recently," Devon whispered back.

Chapter Fourteen

Devon lowered his head, placing soft kisses on the edge of her lips.

Kathleen sighed, his kisses distracting her from his answer. He meant her. She understood his look now. Devon harbored feelings of an intimate nature for her. All these years? How had she not known? Even when he courted Dallis, he gave no indication of holding tender feelings towards Kathleen.

When his mouth hovered over hers, Kathleen raised her face. A question beckoned in his eyes. Devon asked her to meet him halfway. Kathleen crossed the distance and pressed her lips to his. She didn't want to question him or herself. Kathleen only wanted to feel.

Her encouragement was all that Devon needed. He wrapped his arms around Kathleen, bringing her flush alongside him. His kiss devoured her, drawing out each sin that passed between her lips into his. It wasn't enough, Devon desired more.

Devon's passion invaded Kathleen. She'd never imagined he held this desire for her. While she had dreamt of him through the years, his apparent indifference turned her feelings into hatred. To think Devon wished for the same dreams only caused an ache Kathleen yearned for him to relieve.

When he trailed a path of fire along her throat, Kathleen tipped her head back, hoping he would repeat his caresses from Belle's. Her behavior was most wanton for enjoying such a scandalous act, but Kathleen wanted him to love her again. Only this time she wished to please him too.

Kathleen lifted her hand, slowly trailing it down his chest. When she lowered further, Devon stopped her progress with his fingers around her wrist. He closed his eyes as if in pain and stepped back from Kathleen.

Perhaps she was mistaken. Or maybe he preferred a more experienced lady such as Eve or Scarlet. Not Kathleen, an innocent.

Devon watched the doubts enter Kathleen eyes. He wanted her now with a passion he never felt before. But he'd moved too fast. It wasn't his intention when he brought her here today. Devon must return Kathleen home before he raised Rory's ire.

"No, do not put doubt in your mind, my dear. I wish nothing more than to lay you on my bed and make love to you. I feel you perhaps now understand my intentions. I do not want to ruin any chance I may of having of winning your hand with my desires."

Kathleen's doubts vanished at his earnest declaration. She noticed the fear in his eyes that he might scare her away. Also, his hand trembled, and Devon gave himself away by stroking the inside of her wrists. While Devon's words spoke of a need to stop, his caress betrayed a need to touch her.

Kathleen pulled her hand out of his grasp and stepped away from him. She turned her back, setting her hair and dress to rights. When Kathleen turned around again, she gifted him with a shy smile. When Devon relaxed at her acceptance, she decided to tempt him.

"You are correct, my lord." Kathleen wandered closer to the bed, reaching out to stroke the soft silk, her fingers trailing across the bed covers.

She sunk onto the mattress, sighing at the softness. "But aren't wishes meant to be given into?" She propped her head on her arm.

Devon tightened his hands into fists, fighting the desire to join her. His every wish laid before him tempting him, to give into his base desires. Still, Devon stood struggling with his gentlemanly character. Then the scoundrel in him led him forward. When Kathleen undid her hair and her gorgeous mane spread across his covers, it found another chink in the armor of his defense. When she stretched and moaned her delight of his comfortable bed, causing her dress to push her breasts forward, another wall dropped. Devon's gaze trailed to the slim ankles peeking out for his view alone, tempting him. He knew the pleasures that lay hidden underneath that dress.

"Do you not agree, Devon?" Kathleen asked him again.

To hell with being a gentleman. Kathleen was a temptation he wouldn't deny himself. When he drove them here today, the scoundrel in him meant for this very thing to happen. Devon strode to the door, slamming and locking it behind him. On his return to the bed, he divested himself of his coat and cravat. Devon stood above Kathleen, unbuttoning his shirt, and watching the sigh of satisfaction cross her face. He could never refuse her, he understood that now. Even at the threat of both of their demises, he only wished to please her.

"And is this your wish too, my lady?"

Kathleen rose and brushed his hands away. She finished undoing his shirt, pulling it open. Her hands spread out across his chest.

"Yes, it is," she purred.

Kathleen held no clue on how her voice lowered so seductively. She only knew she wanted Devon. She ached to explore what he'd tempted her with before. Would he kiss her so intimately again?

"Then I will take great pleasure at stroking your passions."

Devon turned Kathleen, brushing her hair to the side, kissing her neck while his hands undid her dress. He peeled the dress away, pooling it at their feet. Devon's lips continued their onslaught across her shoulders as he continued to divulge Kathleen of every piece of fabric hiding her body. Once he finished, his gaze took in her backside, then slowly slid her around to take in her full beauty. Kathleen was more beautiful than he even imagined. Devon's dreams paled in the true face of her standing before him.

"You are exquisite."

Kathleen blushed at his stare. Devon's bold assessment spread the blush across her entire body. It also gave Kathleen a confidence she didn't know she possessed. She began to finish what she started and took off his shirt. When she tried to undo his pants he stopped her.

"Another thing I most desire, but unless you wish for this to end before we even begin, then you must allow me."

She didn't want to put a halt on her affections. Kathleen wanted to touch Devon. She saw his hardness pressing against his trousers and knew he wanted her. Kathleen wanted to drive Devon crazier than he did her. She lowered her hand and touched him.

"Kathleen," he growled.

His growl held a sigh too. With a mischievous smile, she continued to undo his trousers.

Kathleen had snuck one of Dallis's romance books into her room upon her return last night. While this wasn't how one would assume a debutante to behave—and she shouldn't have known of this—the book gave every detail on how to pleasure a man. After Devon had pleasured her, Kathleen's curiosity got the better of her, so she read and then read some more. She had hoped to tempt him with this seduction as Scarlet the next time they met. Now this seemed like the perfect opportunity. Her hand slipped inside and cupped his throbbing cock.

Devon moaned at the sweet sensation. Kathleen was a minx set to torture him with her innocence and curiosity. When he could allow no more, Devon lifted Kathleen in his arms and laid her on the bed. He stripped off the rest of his clothing and joined her. Devon paused, staring into Kathleen's eyes.

"I knew you would look gorgeous in blue."

"Devon."

"Yes, love."

"Kiss me."

"With pleasure."

Devon took her mouth in a kiss filled with promises he meant to fulfill. When Kathleen returned them with her own passionate ones, and her hands roamed over his body, Devon lost all rational thought. A need so strong overcame Devon and he could no longer hold himself back.

With every stroke of his tongue, and with every caress of his hand, he staked his claim on Kathleen. Giving neither one of them a trace of doubt.

Devon set Kathleen's body on fire. She clung to him as he worshipped her, whispering endearments as he set her aflame. When he lowered his head between her thighs, his gaze pierced hers. He kissed the inside of her thigh, his lips hovering over her desire. Then he moved away, kissing her other thigh. Kathleen arched her hips when he teased her. Then he moved back, sliding his tongue out for a taste. When Devon moaned his pleasure, he returned to her thigh, brushing a fire in his path. He continued to tease Kathleen, drawing her ache into a need so powerful.

Kathleen's fingers tightened through his hair, and he was aware he'd teased her enough. Her body arched toward his lips. Devon gave into their desires. Kathleen sunk her body into his mouth as he heightened her senses. She opened herself so beautifully to his kisses. Her body responding and building on her ache as he devoured her. Devon sensed Kathleen on the verge of exploding, and slid up her body, between her need.

"Devon," she groaned in frustration.

"When you come, I want to be inside you. I want you to stroke my cock, tightening and squeezing your desire around me."

Devon slid a finger inside Kathleen's pulsing heat. She was ready. He slid in slowly, her body opening to him.

Kathleen never imagined the feelings Devon could stir inside her. The need she held for him continued to own her. When he slid inside her, she felt complete. Still he hesitated. Kathleen ached for him. She wrapped one of her legs around his hip, pressing herself closer. Kathleen brushed her breasts against his chest, her nipples tightening at the contact.

"Devon," she moaned.

"Yes, love."

"Please.

"Please what?"

"Love me."

"With pleasure."

Devon slid deeper inside Kathleen, stretching her to accommodate him. When her body tensed, he didn't move a muscle. Only when she sighed and wrapped herself tight around him did he calm. His Kathleen enraptured him with her beauty and curiosity. When she matched him stroke for stroke, Devon lost the rest of his control.

Kathleen clung to Devon as he made them one. His tenderness when he took her virginity endeared him to her even more. She could tell he kept a tight rein on his desire. However, Kathleen wanted him to come undone with her. She pushed her hips and kissed him with a passion to set him to love her. Kathleen's lips clung to Devon while their passion built to a higher plane. Her hands caressed his body. When still Devon held back, Kathleen whispered in his ear.

"I am yours."

Kathleen's declaration overwhelmed him, and Devon possessed her. His body stroked her higher, and he led them down a path of no return. Their bodies clung to each other when they flew over the edge. His embrace tightened as they gave themselves to each other. Devon still didn't ease his hold when their bodies calmed after the storm.

Only when Kathleen pressed kisses to his neck and chest did he relax. Devon rolled her over and took in her tresses splayed across the pillows. His fingers trailed through them, lost in his thoughts. Kathleen was even more amazing than he had dreamed.

"When we return, I will seek Rory and ask for his permission for your hand."

Kathleen knew he would speak those very words. Even though Devon was a scoundrel, he was also a gentleman. However, Kathleen wasn't finished with her masquerade. She no longer wished to ruin Devon, but she had an end game and needed to finish it. Also, there was the minor issue of her brother no longer considering Devon a friend. Rory detested the man.

"We do not need to rush into marriage. I am only just wrapping my head around your affections."

"I am afraid, my dear, this afternoon we have already rushed our courtship."

"All the more reason to slow it down and let our families grow accustomed to us."

"It is our family's greatest wish for us to wed."

"Our mothers, not my brother or your father."

"That is where you are wrong. My father gave his endorsement a few days ago when he saw you in the garden."

His news didn't really shock Kathleen. Devon's father always spoiled her with candy whenever she visited as a child. He was the one who made it possible for her to have private acting lessons. No, his father wasn't the issue.

"That only leaves Rory."

"I am sure your brother will understand when we explain our need to wed."

"Our need?"

"Yes, Kathleen. I have bedded you, there could be circumstances from our passion."

"Is this the only reason you wish to marry me?"

"No."

"Then please enlighten me to why we need to rush."

"We need to rush because I desire to share my bed with you every night. I desire to kiss you when I please. I desire to stroke you when I want to feel your wetness. I desire to kiss your sweetness endlessly day after day. Night after night. You are my greatest desire and that is why I insist on rushing."

"Oh my, Lord Holdenburg, are you smitten?"

"Yes, Lady Kathleen. With you and only you."

"Well, if you insist."

"I do."

"Very well, but please allow our relationship to develop for a couple of weeks. Take this time to court me and prove to Rory our commitment to one another. Then after two weeks, you can present him with your wishes."

"Our wishes?"

"Our wishes," Kathleen agreed.

Chapter Fifteen

Over the next week, Devon courted Kathleen properly with their mothers' approval. And Rory's disapproval. Every day Devon took her on special outings amongst the ton. He would escort her to luncheons, bring flowers, and dance with her at every ball. His courtship, made known to every gentleman, didn't go unnoticed. And every day Rory would speak his disapproval. Mama kept Rory from interfering, though it was only a matter of time before he would. If Rory didn't come around before the two-week deadline, then he would deny Devon her hand. Kathleen had to convince Rory of her happiness.

Kathleen even stayed away from Belle's. With the attention Devon bestowed upon her, she no longer needed to take revenge. Devon's devotion filled her heart. He found ways for them to be alone where he would steal kisses and whisper how he wanted to make her his again. Every time Kathleen would blush, and he kept making scandalous comments. Their time together couldn't be more perfect.

Even now, with Devon propped against the wall, waiting for her mother to join them, he regarded Kathleen with the exact same stare from when he last escorted them to the theater.

Kathleen asked, "You were never serious about your courtship with Dallis, were you?"

His seductive smile as he pushed himself off and strolled to her gave her his answer before Devon even spoke.

"No, my dear."

He stole a kiss.

"You were in cahoots with my mother even then."

"Yes, my dear."

He stole another kiss.

"Why?"

"Why what?"

"Why did you court Dallis?"

"I owed your mother a favor, and she collected. Plus, I had my own agenda."

"And what might that have been?"

"Why, to make you jealous, my dear."

He stole another kiss before she could say humph.

"Did it work? Were you jealous, my love?"

Kathleen narrowed her eyes as he pulled her into his arms. Devon only laughed. Kathleen attempted to pull away, only for Devon to tighten his hold.

"Well, were you?"

This time Kathleen stole a kiss.

"Tremendously."

Devon tried to steal another kiss, but Kathleen pressed a finger to his lips.

"Why did you owe my mother a favor?"

Devon traced her finger with his tongue. He couldn't answer the question without divulging his deceit. Devon hoped to distract Kathleen with his seduction. He'd enjoyed immensely his week courting Kathleen. Their time together built their attraction to a higher level. Even though he desired to have Kathleen in his bed, strengthening their bond as a couple and giving her a courtship she deserved meant more. However, Devon grew impatient for Rory to accept him in Kathleen's life. His former friend kept a tight grip on his hostility.

Kathleen's eyes softened from his touch, her finger relaxing against his lips. He slowly sucked her finger into his mouth, causing Kathleen to gasp. When she pulled her hand away, Devon closed the gap and took her mouth under his. He kissed her with all the pent-up passion he'd suffered since making love to her. When Kathleen responded so affectionately, he wanted to whisk her away and say to hell with the play.

"That is enough, children. Devon, if you wish to kiss Kathleen so passionately, please find a more discreet hiding place than out in the open for anybody to witness. You are lucky Rory and Dallis have already left."

Kathleen blushed a darker shade of red than Devon had ever seen. Luckily for him, with Lady Beckwith's appearance and his distraction by kissing her, Kathleen had forgotten her question.

"Yes, of course, Lady Beckwith. I will take your advice into serious consideration the next time I steal a kiss from Kathleen."

"Very well, shall we go? Kathleen, dear, please close your mouth before Devon makes us late by kissing it closed. Is your mother waiting in the carriage?"

"Yes, and Father too." Devon stepped away and released Kathleen.

"Excellent, we shall have a grand evening."

"Yes, we shall," Devon replied.

~~~~~~

Devon watched the animation on Kathleen's face from her enjoyment of the performance. Since the play started, he hadn't once taken his eyes off her. And Kathleen's hadn't left the stage. The only moment they did was when he slid their hands together and held them on his lap. It was highly improper, but the darkness allowed this minor act of indecency. Devon needed to touch Kathleen after her playful kisses. They caused him to crave her more.

He felt Rory's glare piercing his back. The man's hatred was fully displayed. The smirk Rory gave him when they entered the box still annoyed Devon. Rory took pleasure on stealing the seats meant for Kathleen and him. Rory commanded the back row with Dallis. When they arrived, everyone had taken their seats, leaving only the front two seats open for them. Rory may have thought him the victor, but it was only for this round. Devon would be the winner in the end.

Devon understood why Rory tried to protect Kathleen. He would have done the same if their situation were reversed. Their longstanding friendship should have been enough proof that Devon's actions were for Kathleen's protection.

Hell, he had fallen for Kathleen years before the fateful night that led him to bet for her. Devon had waited on the sidelines while she matured and enjoyed a few seasons. Because of her father's idiocy, he had to join a wager he wanted no part of. If he hadn't placed a bet, then Kathleen would be the wife of Lord Velden. And Rory wouldn't be able to protect her. Through Devon's chivalry, he lost his best friend and would lose the love of his life if she were to discover the truth.

Devon gripped Kathleen's hand, his frustrations consuming his mind. When she glanced his way with a frown, he loosened his grip. With a smile of assurance, Kathleen turned back to the play. With each day growing closer in requesting Kathleen's hand in marriage, he grew more tense. Devon needed to let off steam. Perhaps a visit to Belle's later this evening would help calm his soul. A few hands of cards and a strong glass of liquid courage. His visits upstairs in the brothel were over. Belle's girls no longer held his interest. Kathleen was enough for him. Belle hadn't sent word of Scarlet visiting her gaming hell. It would appear that whatever sent Kathleen on her path of deception had also ended.

Kathleen's attention shifted from the play at Devon's agitation. The antagonism between Devon and Rory when they arrived didn't go unnoticed. Devon grew angry when her brother smiled smugly at where Dallis and he sat. Devon whispered during the ride of how he wished to spend their time during the play. However, her brother ruined Devon's plans. Kathleen assured him they would find a way for some privacy later. Devon seemed to calm down. But when he gripped her hand so hard, Kathleen wondered if Rory's actions didn't still annoy Devon. His smile tried to reassure her, but the turmoil in his eyes spoke differently.

Kathleen wondered what troubled him. Rory's behavior was the norm for lately, so that wasn't the reason. She tried to immerse herself in the performance, but the play no longer held her interest. Devon did. She turned back and found him staring at her. Throughout the entire evening, while she watched the play, he watched her.

She got lost in Devon's eyes. They pulled her in, drawing her toward an unknown destination. Kathleen didn't care where she ended as long as Devon came with her. When his thumb caressed the inside of her wrist,

Kathleen gasped. They were near the front where anyone would notice if they looked closely enough. That didn't stop Devon. He leaned closer and whispered the most scandalous of thoughts, his eyes never once breaking contact.

If Kathleen didn't stop looking at him like she wished for him to make love to her, he would drag her from the box and find a secluded spot. His family were private donors to the theater. With his parents' love of the stage, he had discovered many secret hiding spots in his youth. Especially when he wished to trifle with the actresses. He knew of a secret place where they wouldn't be found. When Kathleen licked her lips and drew her bottom lip between her teeth, his cock throbbed with an ache only she could relieve.

"My dear, if you do not return your attention to the stage this instant, I can no longer be held responsible for my actions."

Devon slid Kathleen's hand to his lap, laying it on his hardened cock. He hoped his actions would shock her into watching the play. Instead, she spread her fingers wide, molding him to her touch. When her hand gave a gentle squeeze, Devon almost jumped from his seat. Holy hell. What had he started? Kathleen continued to caress him through his trousers, exploring a different way to please him.

Kathleen took great pleasure on how Devon reacted to her touch. He meant to shock her, but he drew out a curiosity she wished to explore. She wanted to touch Devon without all these barriers between them. Before Kathleen continued stroking him, he grabbed her hand and brought it to his lips. He closed his eyes as if in agony when he kissed her knuckles. When he opened them, he racked her with a savage gaze. He laid Kathleen's hand back in her lap and shifted in his seat.

Kathleen meant to tease him some more, but then the candles were lit, and the audience applauded the performance. They even stood to show their approval for an outstanding show. For the first time, Kathleen didn't know how grand it had been. Devon distracted her from her favorite pastime. She couldn't rave about any aspect because Devon consumed her mind.

Kathleen hoped next week would arrive early.

Devon would need more than one drink to remove Kathleen from his mind tonight. How he would endure the rest of the evening would be a true test to his behavior as a gentleman.

"Lord Holdenburg, I have a message for you."

An attendant stood behind him with a note.

Devon, my dear,

I would love to see you after my performance. Please stop by my dressing room before you leave.

Your darling Scarlet,

P.S. And bring along the lovely creature you seem besotted with. You have stroked my interest on who holds your attention so, since obviously it was not my performance.

Devon smiled as he slid the letter inside his suit coat. The actress seemed cross with him. She would get over him soon enough. With the countless chaps always hanging around her dressing room, she wouldn't be lonely for long.

"The lovely Scarlet Nightengale has invited us to her dressing room. Shall we?" Devon asked the group.

The box's enthusiasm at visiting the actress led them all to agree. Devon's father set the lead and everybody followed. Devon lingered near the back, hoping the distraction would allow him a private moment with

Kathleen before anybody noticed their absence. However, it would appear Kathleen held a different view. She joined the group, sharing her excitement with Dallis on getting to meet her favorite performer. Devon hoped Scarlet wouldn't be too annoyed. Her note was only meant for him. The postscript was nothing but a tease. She wanted him alone to continue a past affair which ended a long time ago. But his parents' appearance would soothe Scarlet's bruised ego. She loved when the upper crust of society paid her any kind of attention.

Kathleen would finally get the chance to meet Scarlet Nightengale. When they drew closer to the actress's dressing room, the crowds increased, separating Kathleen from the party. The throngs of theater-goers pushed and shoved. Somebody stepped on the back of her gown, stopping her progress, then suddenly released their hold. Kathleen started falling forward. Before she hit the floor, hands reached out to steady her, and drew her away from the crowd.

Her rescuer led her to a safe place away from the madness. Once they stopped walking, Kathleen looked up to thank her savior. It was none other than Lord Velden.

"It would appear, kind sir, you have rescued me once more."

"After two times, I must deserve an award then."

While his comment should have scared her into finding her family and Devon, it only amused her. She'd enjoyed flirting with him at Belle's and found him harmless, regardless of what Devon said.

"So you do, my lord." Kathleen stepped up on tiptoes and placed a kiss on his cheek.

However, Lord Velden had another intention. He turned his head and her lips brushed against his instead. The move shocked Kathleen and he deepened the kiss. Kathleen didn't return it, and he pulled away. While it wasn't an unpleasant kiss, it didn't compare to Devon.

"Forgive me, my lady, I have overstepped my bounds. In my defense, I could not resist such a sweet temptation. Ever since the Camville ball, you have been in my thoughts. I fear I am smitten."

"I forgive you, my lord." Kathleen believed his words to be true. "However, I hate to disappoint you, but Lord Holdenburg has already made his intentions clear. I fear you are too late."

"Ah, Lord Holdenburg. There is not a man luckier than him. My loss, his gain. Since I have not angered you, may I please escort your return to your family? I cannot leave you alone in this madness."

"Thank you, my lord. Your kindness is most appreciated. I shouldn't tell you this, but your kiss did not bring forth any anger."

"Then if I may so bold as to tell you that the sweetness of your lips is branded on my soul forever."

Kathleen blushed. She didn't know what possessed her to lead Lord Velden on. Perhaps it was the note sent to Devon from the actress. The smile on Devon's face spoke of their past affair. Did their relationship still continue?

When they arrived at the actress's dressing room, all eyes turned toward them. Kathleen rushed into an explanation on how Lord Velden rescued her from the crowd. If she thought the hostility in the box was thick, the air only grew thicker. Rory and Devon both glared at Lord Velden's arrival and the reason behind it. Devon stalked over, inserting himself in between them, his jealousy known to all. However, Kathleen thought it to be more than jealousy. It was almost as if Devon tried to protect her. Or was it himself? He stood on guard, waiting for something to happen. But what?

"Thank you, Lord Velden, for returning Kathleen to us. We owe you debt of gratitude." Even her mother's voice held a stiffness toward the gentleman.

"It was my pleasure. I wish you all a good evening." He bowed toward Kathleen. "As always, my lady, a pleasure."

Kathleen smiled her goodbye, not wanting to draw any more attention to her absence. Devon's mother introduced her to Scarlet Nightengale. Kathleen paid adoration to the beautiful lady. She understood why Devon had been so attracted to her. Not only was she a beauty, but she showed patience to all of Kathleen's questions. Even taking Kathleen for a tour through her costume wardrobe. Before long, they forgot the episode.

On their departure from the dressing room, Scarlet called out, "Devon, dear, may we have a moment?"

Devon paused. He couldn't refuse Scarlet's request without drawing suspicion. However, he didn't want to leave Kathleen's side. Her delay with Lord Velden may appear innocent to some, but Devon knew it was anything but.

Rory clapped Devon on the back, muttering for his ears alone, "Yes, stay and entertain your mistress." To everybody else's ears he said, "Mother and Kathleen can ride home with us. There is no need for two carriages to convey us to the same destination."

"Yes, that would be best. It has been an entertaining evening. Thank you, Your Graces, for your wonderful invitation. We shall see you tomorrow, Lord Holdenburg," Lady Beckwith replied.

With that, Devon watched Kathleen leave without even saying goodbye. What a way to end what he'd hoped would be a different evening. Now he must extract himself from Scarlet.

"Yes, my dear?" He turned toward her.

"Now, why such a sour tone?" Scarlet's lips pulled into a pout.

Devon didn't answer. He didn't want to lead her on. When he showed no interest, she sauntered toward him, brushing against him. When Devon still didn't move, Scarlet turned around.

"Can you at least unbutton my dress?"

Devon sighed and released the hooks. Scarlet turned back around, the gown falling off her shoulders. She slid her hands through the sleeves and pushed it off her waist. Her dress pooled around her feet. She wore nothing but a transparent chemise. When Scarlet tried to kick her dress away, she lost her balance and grabbed for Devon. He snatched her around the waist. She purred with delight at being held in his embrace and tightened her arms around him. Once he had regained her balance, he tried to get out of Scarlet's clutches, but she wouldn't release him. Scarlet started pulling his head down for a kiss.

"Please forgive me, I forgot my program—" Kathleen stood wide-eyed in the doorway.

"Kathleen, you cannot rush—" Rory stopped behind Kathleen.

Devon pushed Scarlet from his arms, but it was too late. The damage had already been done. Kathleen eyes filled with a hurt, tearing at his gut. Even though he was innocent, it didn't matter, for it appeared he'd trifled with Scarlet. Still, he tried to convince Kathleen otherwise.

"Kathleen, please let me explain. This is all a misunderstanding."

He tried to place his hands on Kathleen's shoulders. Rory pulled her out of his reach. Kathleen wouldn't meet Devon's eyes.

Rory snapped, "You have done enough, Holdenburg. I tried to prevent this. I even went along with my mother and Dallis's wishes on allowing you

to court Kathleen. You have only proven my opinion correct. At least
Kathleen has seen for herself the scoundrel you are."

"Kathleen?" Devon ignored Rory.

"Kathleen, let's go. Do not follow us, Holdenburg."

Rory pulled Kathleen away, and they disappeared down the hallway,
lost in the crowd.

Devon spun around. "What in the hell was that scene for?"

"How was I supposed to know your little baggage would return?"

"Do not refer to her as *that*," Devon snarled.

Scarlet rolled her eyes, drawing on a robe, realizing she would get
nowhere with Devon this evening.

"What did you need?" he asked.

"I thought we could pick up where we left off."

"Well, you thought wrong. We were finished years ago."

"You will never find happiness with someone as simple as her."

"I was not aware I asked for your opinion. Scarlet, let me make myself
clear, our relationship is finished. I wish you well on your career."

Devon left. He wanted no more inconveniences this evening and Scarlet
Nightengale was an inconvenience. He only wanted to follow Kathleen
home and beg for her forgiveness. When he explained himself, he hoped
Kathleen trusted him enough to know he spoke the truth. In the end though,
any attempt he made would only be for naught. Rory would make sure
Devon never stepped foot in their home again. And he couldn't blame him.

Which only left one place for him to drink his sorrows away. Belle's.

~~~~~

Kathleen trudged up the stairs to her bedroom. Even when her mother called out, she continued. She had been numb since she saw Devon holding the scantily clad actress. After seeing him clutching the beauty in his arms, with their lips almost connecting, Kathleen didn't remember a thing. Except for the ride home. Where Rory went on a tirade about Devon's character, slandering him. When Kathleen never responded, he became angrier. Even Mama and Dallis's soothing words didn't penetrate her fog. She closed the bedroom door to block out her brother's rants.

She curled up on the divan near the window and stared out into the darkness. The evening had started out perfectly and now ended with such deep sorrow. The scene she walked in on spoke for itself. Kathleen should have known better. Devon would never be faithful.

A knock sounded at the door. When Kathleen didn't answer, Dallis slid inside and closed the door behind her. She came over to Kathleen, sitting beside her.

"Would you like to talk, dear?"

Kathleen shook her head.

"Rory informed us what you witnessed. I am positive Devon has an explanation."

"On how he is a worthless bastard who will bed any harlot that will spread her thighs for him?"

"Kathleen, you have to be mistaken. Devon loves you."

"He has spoken no words of love."

"I only ask this of you, when he calls tomorrow, for he will, please listen to him. If after he has spoken you do not believe him, then end your relationship. Please, give him a chance to explain."

Kathleen didn't answer, turning her head to stare into the night. She understood Dallis meant well. But Dallis held a close friendship with Devon. Kathleen had observed their courtship, envious of her sister-in-law, and Devon had been very protective of Dallis.

Eventually Dallis left her alone. Kathleen determined she wouldn't shed a tear for Devon. Her heart was aware of who he was. Why Kathleen thought he had changed, she held no clue. It would appear the scoundrel charmed even her. Well, no more. A few weeks ago she set out to destroy him, but he'd distracted her with affection. Which she now knew to be false.

Kathleen rose and set out to her nightly designation. She only hoped she didn't run across Devon there. She wanted to be alone. Maybe Lord Velden would be there to entertain her. Kathleen remembered their time alone at the theater. He did her ego good. And his kiss was quite pleasant enough. He took a liking to her Scarlet too, and perhaps Scarlet could entice Velden. Kathleen would do anything to wipe away the memory of Holdenburg clutching the actress to his body. It would seem his appetite was insatiable. Kathleen would never have been enough for Devon.

Chapter Sixteen

Devon started off in the bar, drinking his sorrows away. After he finished one bottle, he carried another one with him to play cards. Who could he destroy this evening? He found a table full of young pups and set about taking their money from them one by one. When he cleared out the last young gentleman, he moved to the next table. Devon hoped their rotten luck would make them think twice before blowing their money on something out of their control. The next table became a little more difficult to win. He thought he lost more hands than he won. Since his pile of chips hadn't diminished, he continued to play.

Even when the cards became blurry, he didn't quit. Devon only called Eve over to help him out. The blonde slid onto his lap, her breasts brushing his chest every time she whispered the cards into his ear. He had divested himself of his coat, vest, and cravat. Only a thin white shirt lay between them. Eve's tight nipples scraped him at every twist and turn of her body. Every time she helped him win a hand, he would thank her with a kiss, each kiss placed in an inviting spot. Kathleen was such a minx to tease him like this. He should cover her body.

His mind kept playing tricks with him. He saw that it was Eve who rested on his lap, but he couldn't get Kathleen out of his mind.

When he bested the table, he tried to move to another one, but nobody wished for him to join them. So Devon sat drinking more while fondling the creature in his lap. When he placed his lips on Eve's neck, he thought he kissed Kathleen. When his hands slid inside Eve's shift, cupping her breast, he thought he held Kathleen's beautiful globes. When Eve sighed and pushed her bottom on his cock, he thought it was the whisper of Kathleen sighing and his cock hardened. His grip tightened on her breast, twisting her nipple. Devon slipped his hand between Eve's thighs and brushed across her wetness. He had to have her now. He rose, grabbing her hand, and stopped. It was not Kathleen's hand he held, for she stood just inside the doorway talking to Belle, her stare penetrating him. Oh, holy hell. While he was innocent from before, he was guilty as hell now.

~~~~~~

While it was painful to watch Devon fondle the harlot on his lap, it confirmed Kathleen's opinion of him. He had played her false for the last time.

"He does not even realize who sits in his lap," Belle tried to reassure her.

"It does not matter."

"I think it does, by the sign of your tightened fists."

"Lord Holdenburg can bed every available or unavailable female in Christendom, for all that I care."

"What has happened? I have not seen you, and the rumor mill suggests that Holdenburg will propose soon."

"Rumors are all they were."

"Kathleen," Belle whispered.

"Scarlet."

"Please come to my parlor. You are witnessing a man who has drank two bottles of my finest whiskey and does not remember his own name."

"But he knows enough to win at cards? I see his winnings and I wish to play with him. Can you arrange a game?"

"Yes," Belle sighed.

Belle shook her head at the young lady's determination. Holdenburg had gotten himself in a fine mess now. Why was he fooling around with Eve? Something must have occurred for the change in their relationship. When Lady Kathleen had ceased visiting her establishment in the dead of night, and with Devon's absence, she inquired to their whereabouts. When her friends confirmed Devon escorting Kathleen around town, Belle felt reassured that they would soon make an announcement on their upcoming nuptials. But this evening's activities showed there would be no wedding, only heartache for both parties.

Belle walked over to Devon's table, expressing her disgust at his behavior. When he arched his eyebrow, Belle glared at him. If he thought to intimidate her with his superior rank, then she would have him thrown out on his arse right this instant. So she arched her brow right back at him. His expression changed to apologetic, but it was too late. Belle's patience wore thin with these tiring men. Every single one of them had an amazing woman within their grasp, and they ruined it with their arrogant ways.

"Lady Scarlet wishes to play a game of cards with you. Do you accept her request?"

Devon spread his arms wide for Scarlet to join him at the table. So the lady wanted to play. He should send Eve away, but he had already passed hell and couldn't return. Also, if Kathleen held such a lack of faith in his character, their relationship no longer mattered. Obviously, she never trusted him.

"Lord Holdenburg."

"Lady Scarlet."

Kathleen raised her brow at Eve sitting on his lap. Devon wrapped his arm tighter around Eve and pulled her closer. Eve snuggled into him, moaning. Her hands roamed his body, staking her claim.

"Eve here is my lucky charm this evening. She holds faith in me."

"Silly girl," Devon heard Kathleen mutter.

Before they could begin playing, Lord Velden walked behind Kathleen and rested his hands on her shoulders. Devon wanted to rise and slam him to the floor. He had the audacity to touch his woman. When Velden sent him a look, Devon realized Lord Velden knew that Kathleen and Scarlet were the same lady. Devon couldn't say a word or it would jeopardize Kathleen's identity to everybody else in the room.

"I have missed you, my lady." Lord Velden spoke near Kathleen's ear.

Kathleen turned and bestowed the lord with a seductive smile.

"And I you, my lord."

"May I join you?"

"I am sorry, I have promised a private game with Lord Holdenburg."

"Perhaps another time then? May I have a private word with you before you begin?"

"By all means, my lord."

Devon watched Velden lead Kathleen towards a darkened corner. His anger escalated when Velden pulled Kathleen close and whispered in her ear. Then his lips trailed along her neck and Kathleen tilted her head for him to gain better access. The whole time she never broke eye-contact with

Devon. Her gaze dared him to object. When Lord Velden's lips trailed to her breasts, Devon dropped Eve off his lap onto the floor and stepped forward. He would tear Velden limb from limb. When Eve whined her discomfort, Velden raised his head and chuckled. The lord whispered something to make Kathleen laugh. They both turned to stare at him.

"I think you dropped your piece of baggage, Holdenburg." Velden baited him.

"Are we playing cards this evening, Lady Scarlet? If not, I have a more pressing matter to attend to," Devon asked as he helped Eve off the floor, settling her once more on his lap.

"Yes, Lord Holdenburg, I believe we shall. Lord Velden, I promise this Saturday evening, I am all yours. Perhaps, after our card game, we can partake of more pleasurable pursuits?" Kathleen spoke loud enough for Devon to hear. If he would throw his conquests in her face, then she would do the same to him.

"I wait in anticipation, my dear." He kissed her knuckles before strolling away. But not before he sent Devon a victory look.

Kathleen returned to the table. She was too calm. Not one ounce of hurt or betrayal crossed her features. Not even revenge. Nor jealousy. Kathleen ignored Eve as if she didn't cling to Devon. She played her hands of cards. Winning some, losing some. Neither of them bending to the other. Throughout their card game, Devon tried to draw a reaction from her, but nothing. Even when Devon fondled Eve, Kathleen didn't react.

"I guess the rumors surrounding you are true, my lord?"

"And those would be?"

"Oh, the ones where you are a drunk, gambler, and a scoundrel to all women."

"A reputation I have taken years to perfect."

"I think you have perfected them. Although I feel for the young miss I have seen you escorting around town. Lady Kathleen, is it not?"

So she wished to play her hand this way, did she? Devon would play along, and perhaps he could convince Kathleen of his innocence.

"You are correct. I plan to ask her brother for her hand next week."

"Why wait?"

"It was per her request."

"It is a shame somebody as elegant as Lady Kathleen does not satisfy your sexual cravings. You men are all alike."

"Do not lump me in the same pile as your poor excuse of a husband, my lady."

"Please tell me how you are any different. He now lies between his mistress's legs and you are sitting with yours on your lap right now. What would Lady Kathleen say if she were to witness your behavior? I think it would hurt her, the innocent that she is."

Kathleen's words cut through Devon. He was as guilty as her fictitious husband. He had no excuse except for being stinking drunk and imagining Eve was Kathleen. Devon's disgust for himself sat in his gut. He didn't reply. However, Kathleen was far from finished.

"I only hope you have not told the poor girl that you love her. For when she discovers your extra-marital pursuits, it will hurt her deeply. No, it is best you enter your relationship with no words of affection. Believe me, it will be much easier for her in the long run."

Devon stilled. He'd never told Kathleen he loved her. What a damn fool he was. If he did, then Kathleen would never had doubted him and would have trusted that he didn't fool around with Scarlet Nightengale. True, he called her dear and my love, but he never spoke the exact words. Now he feared he'd lost her.

Devon kept drinking, becoming more depressed. His words slurred as he tried to provoke her, but still nothing. When she depleted him of his entire winnings of the night, she rose and thanked him for a most enlightening evening. Her prim and proper, polite mannerisms grated across his nerves.

When she left, he followed. Before he crossed into the hallway, Belle stepped in front of him.

"Leave her be, Devon."

"Do not stand in my way, Madame."

"If you follow her, you will forever live to regret your actions."

"If I do not follow, I will regret that I did not."

Belle stepped to the side when she noted the desperation in his eyes. She followed at a discreet distance, watching Devon stride into Kathleen's room. He slammed the door behind him. Belle took up the position of guard, ready to enter if she heard any distress from Kathleen. Belle knew in her heart Devon would never hurt her, but with being so deep into his bottles of whiskey, she didn't know what his intentions were. When people hurt, they react emotionally before thinking through on their words or actions. Inside that room were two people whose hearts ached.

"Well, my lady, you played an excellent hand of cards this evening."

"I wish I could return the compliment, my lord, but I cannot."

Kathleen knew Devon would follow her. As they played cards, she noticed how despondent he became. Devon appeared as if his entire world fell apart at his feet. Her heart ached for him. Why was she so vulnerable to him? She even watched how he betrayed her with Eve. It was almost as if he provoked her on purpose. Devon wanted her to react, and she didn't. Kathleen's emotions were too numb.

Devon stalked toward her, causing Kathleen to back up until she hit the wall.

"You cheated," he claimed.

"You, sir, are drunk."

"Yes, I am. But I know when I am being cheated, and you cheated on every hand you won."

Kathleen tried pushing Devon away, but her strength was no match for him. He pressed closer.

"There is only one way for you to walk out of here without having me inform Belle of your antics. Belle does not take kindly to cheaters. She will not welcome you here again. Such a shame too, since you have made plans with Lord Velden on Saturday evening."

Devon had her. She *had* cheated while she played. She figured as drunk as he was, he would be easy prey. Each hand the dealer gave her were losers. Kathleen had to cheat to win. She couldn't allow Devon to call her out. Kathleen needed to play that card game with Lord Velden.

"Perhaps we can come to an agreement, Lord Holdenburg?" Kathleen lowered her voice seductively and trailed her fingers over his shirt buttons. She slowly slid each button out of their holes. Her hand laid on his bare chest, her fingers caressing him.

Devon lost all sense when Kathleen touched him. He ached to be inside her. He pulled her to him and ravaged her lips. She returned his kiss not as the innocent Kathleen, but as the experienced Scarlet. With each thrust of his tongue, she battled with him. Her fingers scratched down his chest, their kiss consuming each other.

Kathleen only meant to tease him enough so he wouldn't tell her secret. She never imagined he would unleash this undeniable passion. Devon made her body ache for him. She wanted to lash at him with anger, and instead melted at his touch. Kathleen would cut all ties with Devon after this night. But Scarlet could have him. For one more night, Kathleen could love Devon. Then Kathleen could move on. She would forget her past and recover from her heartache. Kathleen knew she'd provoked Devon about words of love never spoken. But she was just as guilty. She never told Devon how much she loved him. How she still did. No matter how much he hurt her, he would always hold her heart.

"I want you," Devon moaned against her lips.

Kathleen laughed bitterly. "You want any woman to satisfy your urges. I am no fool, my lord. I know I am only a body to be used."

He grabbed the back of her head, staring into her eyes and spoke vehemently. "No, I only want you. You are the only one I have ever wanted. And you are the only one who I will ever want."

Devon's passionate speech shook Kathleen. He spoke from the soul. Which hurt her all the more. Devon had never wanted Kathleen—not if he spoke of his desire for *Scarlet* this way. But Kathleen was lost and couldn't deny herself the pleasures of his arms one last time.

Kathleen's answer was to slide his shirt off. Then she lowered herself to her knees and undid the buttons on his trousers. When she slid his pants down, his cock sprang out, hard and ready. She slid her hand around him, slowly stroking the velvet smooth cock. When he groaned, Kathleen looked up and saw the need in Devon's eyes. She trailed her tongue along the length to the tip where her tongue swirled, licking at his juices, her eyes never once leaving his. When her mouth lowered, taking him inside, he closed his eyes, groaning. Kathleen stroked him in and out, while his hands glided through her hair, holding her.

"Ah love," he moaned.

Hearing the pleasure in his voice, Kathleen increased the pressure as she sucked him harder. She drew him deeper into her mouth. His cock throbbed his need in her mouth, making her ache to her core. Kathleen wanted him inside her.

Kathleen rose and removed her dress. This time she wore nothing beneath. It was as if she knew this would be the outcome to her evening. Had Kathleen hoped for this to happen? Is that why she continued with this madness?

Devon watched Kathleen's dress fall. She wore not a stitch under her clothing. She stood proudly before him with her head held high. Devon's gaze traveled the length of her body. Kathleen's breasts were full, and her nipples tightened at his stare. Her stomach was flat and her hips flared. Kathleen's black curls beckoned him closer, but still Devon didn't touch her. Her long glorious legs begged him to—oh, how he wanted them around his waist.

"You are exquisite."

Devon dropped to his knees. He kissed each thigh as they opened for him. Her wet core beckoned him. He ran his tongue across her, teasing her clit. He pulled back. Devon slid a finger inside her.

"You consume my thoughts." His finger slid in and out.

Devon slid in another finger. "My body aches for you." He drew out each caress.

"My mouth waters for a taste of your sweetness." Devon's tongue stroked her, drawing out her desires drop by drop.

Kathleen's legs almost buckled from the onslaught of Devon's pleasure. His wicked mouth devoured her while his fingers played her body with a skill only he would ever hold over her. With each stroke, her body ached to explode. Devon lifted her leg over his shoulder, pressing his mouth deeper, sliding his tongue in and out with his fingers. Kathleen drew his head closer, losing control. She ached for him—needing Devon to erase her heartache.

He pulled away and she whimpered. He drew up her body, wrapping her legs around his hips and plowed into her with one thrust.

"You are the very breath of my soul."

His body rocked into hers over and over as they clung to each other. She met each of his thrusts.

Kathleen screamed his name as their bodies became one. She undid him. She possessed him mind, body, and soul. There would never be another for him.

Kathleen clung to Devon as he loved her. She never wanted to let go. His grip tightened as he pulled her close. He carried them to the couch, collapsing with her held to his chest.

Kathleen brushed the hair from his eyes. "Lord Holdenburg, why did you drink so heavily tonight?"

Devon sighed. Even after the passion they shared, she still wanted to keep up the pretense.

"I had hoped to wipe the memory of Lady Kathleen's heartache from my mind."

"And did you?"

"No, there is not enough alcohol for that, believe me. I have tried many times."

Devon grew sleepy and with the effects of the spirits he became even more confused.

"Tried what many times?"

"To forget her."

"Why did you want to forget her?"

"Because when she discovers my secret, I will lose her anyway."

"What is your secret?"

Kathleen's question went unanswered. Devon fell fast asleep. Even though he wasn't awake, he never relaxed his hold. His grip tightened in sleep, as if he feared losing her.

"I do not understand you, Devon. You speak of hurting me, yet you poured your heart out to Scarlet. I know I speak a quandary, since we are the same. But you do not realize that. I may hold your affection, but it is Scarlet who holds your passion for life. Your love. How I envy her."

Kathleen pressed her lips against his and moved out from underneath his arms. She continued to watch him as she dressed. Devon would suffer greatly when he awoke. Even more so when he called on Kathleen tomorrow. Devon broke her heart, now Kathleen would have to break his.

When she closed the door, Belle stepped out of the shadows.

"Are you finished? Have you gotten your revenge?"

"No, I will finish on Saturday evening. The men who destroyed my father will suffer their own demise."

"I feel after this evening, one of them already has."

"He deserved no less."

"You are incorrect, my lady. He did not deserve any of it and one day you will realize that. I only hope it will not be too late for you."

"He destroyed my family."

"No, he *saved* your family."

"You do not know what you speak."

"I know more than you do. If you do not believe me, ask him yourself."

"I no longer trust him."

"Then ask your mother."

"My mother?"

"Yes, my lady. I will have Ned escort you home himself."

Kathleen watched Belle move away. Belle defended Holdenburg as if he were a saint. Another one who had fallen for his charms. Just like her mother. She couldn't ask her mother about Devon. Because like every other lady, he'd bowled her over with his charisma. Her mother thought Devon walked on water and would never speak ill of him.

Chapter Seventeen

Kathleen hadn't expected Devon so early in the morning. After he had imbibed so much at Belle's bar, she expected him later in the day. When Agnes knocked on her door, Kathleen dressed and hurried downstairs. No need to prolong the inevitable. Also, she needed to get rid of Devon before Rory came down. While Kathleen was finished with Devon, she didn't wish to see him hurt or—as furious as Rory was—even killed.

Kathleen had pulled on an old day dress, because she planned on helping Mama in the garden later. When she glanced in the mirror, her bedraggled appearance stared back. With a sigh, she sat at the beauty table. She continued to stare at the woman in the mirror. The sadness in her eyes showed only a small part of what tore her apart. Kathleen brushed her hair and pulled the long strands into a bun. A few tendrils slipped out and clung to her neck. Her cheeks were pale, so she pinched them, bringing forth a bit of color. It would have to do. She no longer wanted to please Devon anyway. Last night showed her proof of his devotion to Scarlet. Kathleen may have been passable to appease their mothers, but she wasn't enough to satisfy him. Devon would always seek another.

Devon paced back and forth in the Beckwith parlor. He'd called on Kathleen as early as it was fashionably accepted. She was an early riser and today would be no different. Her pride wouldn't allow her to lie about in bed all day. No, Kathleen would appear to all that life was perfect. She would bury the hurt deep.

She wouldn't expect him so soon. Devon surprised himself with his early arrival. With the amount of alcohol he drank last night, he should spend the day in bed. But alcohol didn't hold the same effect on him like most men. He'd learned in his youth that he had an iron stomach. The more he drank, the more it held no impact on him. Hell, he was surprised he remembered anything from the night before. He not only remembered; the visions were seared into his brain. Devon replayed them over and over until the need to see Kathleen grew stronger. Devon didn't care how early it was. Kathleen must give him another chance.

"Hello, Lord Holdenburg. To what do we owe this early morning arrival?"

"I had hoped you would allow me to explain what you imagined you witnessed at the theater last night."

"I have no need to listen to your false excuses. What I witnessed was explanation enough."

"They are not false."

"Your actions showed your true character, my lord. One that I am glad I witnessed before you spoke to Rory."

"Kathleen, you misunderstand."

"I misunderstand nothing, Lord Holdenburg. I understand you are a drunken scoundrel who will never find satisfaction with one woman. You will always crave another. Someone who can scratch an itch that I cannot. I no longer wish to associate myself with a gentleman never truly devoted to me. I want a man who cherishes me as his entire universe. And you, sir, are not that man."

Kathleen allowed her heartache to speak.

Devon needed to show Kathleen she was incorrect. He was that man. There was no other but her. And her alone. He slid an arm around her shoulders, bringing her flush with his body. Kathleen held herself stiff, turning her head to the side, refusing to look at him. He twined his finger in a loose curl. Devon itched to release the rest of her hair. To allow the locks to fall over her shoulders so he could run his hands through them.

"Love, please look at me."

Kathleen almost gave in to the desperation in Devon's voice. His pain echoed in her soul. She only had to turn her head. But if Kathleen did, she would fall for the falsity in his gaze. She refused to believe in him, his searching gaze, his sensual voice, but most of all his touch. Everything there was about him.

"Kathleen," he pleaded.

Devon pulled her closer, his lips brushing the curl. Kathleen closed her eyes. She needed to move away. But the pull of their connection kept her still. Devon laid his head on her shoulder; she felt the dejection. Devon seemed to be sincere. Kathleen almost fell for it. Then she remembered her Scarlet clutching at him. Kathleen remembered what he said to Scarlet as he filled her last night. When he took possession of her body for the final time. His words, "You are the very breath of air to my soul." His words were spoken to another woman, not her.

Kathleen stepped back and Devon dropped his arms. While she'd started to soften toward him, at the last minute he lost her. He wanted to say what she meant to him, but she needed time. The events from the previous evening were too raw. Perhaps, in a few days time, he could convince

Kathleen of his innocence. In the meantime, he would attempt every day to win her love back.

"I realize you do not want to listen to my excuses. But I want you to understand how deeply sorry I am, if any of my actions have hurt you. I never meant to cause you any pain."

Kathleen wanted Devon to leave. Once again she was numb to her emotions. She didn't know how to deal with a vulnerable Devon. Perhaps, another day, she could hear his explanations. But for now, she wanted him gone.

"Please leave, Devon."

All Devon could do was to honor her request. When she finally spoke his name, not Lord Holdenburg, it gave him hope that Kathleen still held feelings for him. He wanted to stay and find out. But Devon heard Kathleen's pain when she spoke.

"Good day, Kathleen. I will not say goodbye, because I will return tomorrow. If you refuse my visit, then I shall call the next, and the day after that. One day you will speak to me."

Devon walked out the door, leaving the woman he loved behind. His heart rate increased as his steps took him further away. He would need to curb his desire to stay, and allow for Kathleen's heartache to subside.

Kathleen curled up in the chair next to the window, watching Devon stride down the sidewalk. When he reached his carriage, he glanced back at the house. Without realizing it, Kathleen rested her hand on the window glass as if she were reaching out to him. When Devon took a step forward, Kathleen pulled her hand away. Before the curtain closed, she saw the hurt in his gaze. Devon nodded to Kathleen and climbed inside, driving away.

Tears streamed down Kathleen's face as she wrapped her arms around herself. They were a sad replacement for Devon's arms. She still felt the desperation of his hold. Why did he act so hurt when she was the one who suffered heartache? Kathleen laid her head on the arm of the chair, her feet tucked underneath, pouring her heart out. She missed him already. She could easily forgive him. However, she wouldn't live her life like her mother. Mother was naïve and hadn't been aware of Father's infidelity until his death. The man she loved had fooled her. Kathleen could by no rights enter a union already knowing her husband would stray. She wouldn't be able to handle the heartache. Kathleen would always wonder whose company he kept. When he was with her, would his thoughts turn to another? Kathleen wouldn't allow her peers to laugh behind her back or pity her. No, she wouldn't endure that life.

"Kathleen, love, are you well?" Dallis spoke near her.

"Devon was here."

Rory said, "Where is the bastard? He dared to step foot in our home after last night?" He turned toward the door, ready to storm after Devon.

"He is long gone."

Rory hunched in front of her, drawing her hands into his.

"Did he hurt you?"

"If the pain is so powerful it leaves you numb, then yes, he hurt me. I loved him, Rory. Not the simple infatuation kind of love, but the same love you share with Dallis. The kind where he holds my heart in the palm of his hands and guards it for safekeeping. But he did not hold it carefully enough, for he has dropped it and my heart has shattered to pieces."

Rory pulled Kathleen in and held her. She cried out her heartache in his arms. When they were younger, Rory would find ways to torment her. He took great pride in being the older brother who teased his little sister. But if anybody *else* ever hurt Kathleen, he always picked her up and held her, protecting Kathleen from harm. When their father died, he did everything in his power to keep protecting her. But with Devon Holdenburg he'd failed tremendously. He let Dallis and his mother convince him to allow their relationship to play itself out, and Kathleen came away in tears. Kathleen had fallen deeper in love with Devon over the last few weeks. Hell, he even thought his old friend might harbor the same feelings. But as usual, Holdenburg proved himself to be the scoundrel the ton painted him out to be. Kathleen believed herself in love with Holdenburg in her younger years. She would trail after the two boys, always catering to Holdenburg's whims. When Kathleen began regarding Holdenburg with hostility, Rory thought she had outgrown her fascination. Kathleen noticed how Holdenburg devoured the women of the ton like they were candy. Then, when he courted Kathleen like a proper gentleman, Rory gave Holdenburg the benefit of doubt that he had changed.

Hell, Holdenburg courted Dallis better than Rory did. Rory should have known better. As soon as Dallis disregarded Holdenburg, he moved on to Kathleen. Why did Holdenburg court Kathleen? The only explanation that came to Rory's mind was that Holdenburg meant to collect on that damned bet. Rory would never allow that to happen. Rory considered the bet void on his father's death.

Rory tipped Kathleen's chin up. "You may hurt now, but in time you will forget this brief episode and move on to greater things. I promise."

Kathleen hugged Rory. He was her rock. She always depended on him. Every man in her life failed her, but Rory never did. He'd sacrificed much for their family, even his own happiness. Kathleen no longer wished to be a burden on him. Rory carried too many responsibilities in life. Now Dallis and him were expecting a baby. He didn't need to worry about her. Kathleen needed to reassure him.

"As always, brother, you are correct. Lord Holdenburg is but one gentleman in a ballroom of many. I shall try to remove him from my heart and open myself to another gentleman more worthy."

Dallis watched Kathleen agree with her brother too easily. While she adored Kathleen, the girl would portray to her family that she was fine when she was anything but. The heartache shone in Kathleen's eyes, and she would never forget Devon Holdenburg. Kathleen only spoke those words to Rory so he wouldn't go after Devon. That alone spoke how much Kathleen cared for Devon. She lied to her brother to save Devon from Rory's brutal fists.

Dallis decided she must talk to Devon. There was a missing plot to this story. The friend Dallis came to know would never have done what Rory and Kathleen accused him.

After Kathleen assured Rory that she would be all right, Rory left for Lord Hartridge's. This left Dallis alone with Kathleen, who she regarded with a shrewdness that made Kathleen uncomfortable. Kathleen smoothed her hands down her dress and rose to make an excuse to retire to her room.

"Before you leave, will you please answer a few questions for me?" asked Dallis.

Kathleen sighed, she could never deny Dallis anything. When Rory married Dallis, she gained the sister she never had and always wanted. Kathleen suspected Dallis would ask questions regarding Devon. Questions that Kathleen wouldn't be able to answer with lies. Perhaps she should confide in Dallis about her late night visits and swear her to secrecy? Belle had suggested Kathleen ask her mother about Devon's character, suggesting that her mother held secrets. But Kathleen refused. Perhaps Dallis would confide in her? Surely, Rory didn't keep any secrets from Dallis. Yes, Dallis was the key to the answers she needed.

"What do you wish to know?"

"What happened at the theater to ignite Rory's temper? Did Devon betray you?"

"When I ran back to collect my program, I found Devon holding Scarlet in his arms. She clung to him, wearing nothing but a thin chemise."

"And Devon?"

"I already told you, he was holding her."

"Was Devon fully clothed?"

Where were Dallis's questions leading? Of course, Devon had his clothes on. There wasn't a stitch out of place on him.

"Yes."

"And how was he holding her? Were they in a passionate embrace? Were they kissing? Did his hands roam her nearly naked body?"

The answer to all her questions was nay.

"No."

"Perhaps you are mistaken? Maybe Devon is innocent of what Rory and you accuse him?"

Was he? Did Kathleen misinterpret what she saw?

"Can I tell you what I observed last night?" When Kathleen nodded, Dallis continued. "We sat behind you at the theater, and Devon regarded you the same way that he regarded you when he courted me. I watched a man staring at a woman he adored, enjoying her favorite pastime. Then later, the very same man became upset when you had gotten lost on the way to Scarlet's dressing room. When you waltzed in with Lord Velden, Holdenburg held back from expressing his jealously. Then I saw him stay by your side with a need to not be apart from you.

I also watched Scarlet shooting daggers at you, her jealously made clear to everybody but you, because you could not see past your awe of her as your favorite actress. She played on your kindness to pretend that she held no ulterior motives when she invited Devon to her dressing room. She was furious that he brought his entire party with him. Her invitation was meant for him alone."

Kathleen reconsidered what she'd walked in on. Oh, no she was *wrong*. Devon was innocent. Now she remembered how Devon didn't have his hands on Scarlet Nightengale. The actress clung to him, but he held himself stiffly away. The expression on Devon's face was one of impatience. Kathleen realized what a fool she'd had been. What had she done?

But still, that didn't excuse Devon from later, when he seduced her as Scarlet. Devon may not have cheated on her with Scarlet the actress, but he had with Scarlet, the lady from Belle's.

"I wronged him by not listening to his explanation. But it does not matter, for he betrayed me later with another lady."

"Who and where? How do you know of his betrayal?"

Kathleen sighed. "Where is Mama?"

"She is helping Agnes in the kitchen."

Kathleen rose and closed the door to the parlor and sat next to Dallis.

"Will you promise to keep the secret I am about to confide to you? You must swear you will never fill Rory's ears with it."

"I promise, Kathleen."

"I have been sneaking out of the house and visiting a brothel with a gaming hell connected to it. The establishment is owned by a lady named—"

"Belle. Yes, I am well aware of the place. Your brother used to fight there."

"He told you everything about the establishment?"

"Yes, it was hard to keep it a secret when he came home bloody and beaten shortly after we were married."

"Yes, well, Belle admitted my entry to the gaming hell. It was my intention to ruin the two men who brought about my father's demise."

"Explain yourself, Kathleen."

"I'm not sure of all the details, but Lord Velden and Lord Holdenburg drew my father into a game that made him gamble away his remaining fortune. If it were not for these gentlemen, then father would still be alive. After the game, he turned to drinking heavily, and his heart gave out on him. I intend to make them pay, especially Holdenburg. The last card game, he came away the victor. Holdenburg stole everything from my father."

"Then why have you allowed Holdenburg to court you, if your only goal was to ruin him?"

"Because like every other woman, I fell for his charm. I thought he cared about me, but after last night I realized it was all a pretense. I will never be enough for him."

"Kathleen, you must have an honest discussion with Devon. There are many aspects you do not understand."

"Do you? Belle suggested that I ask Mama about Devon, but Mama favors him and would never speak ill of him."

"No, I do not. When Devon courted me, he hinted of a secret. Rory has never confided in me why he detests Devon. There must be an explanation on what occurred during that card game."

"What could that be?"

"I do not know, my dear, but I mean to find out. In the meantime, please continue your explanation on how Devon could never be faithful to you."

"Because I have knowledge that he made love to another woman at Belle's."

"And how would you know that?"

"Because I am that woman."

"Kathleen, please be more specific."

"For me to play cards there, Belle gave me the use of her collection of masks to hide my identity. During my time there I went by the name of Scarlet and always wore a mask."

"And you think Devon held no clue it was you?"

"No, he gave no sign."

"Mmm."

"He didn't, Dallis. And he pursued Scarlet like he never pursued Kathleen. The passion he showed was nothing compared to the passion we shared. Their attraction exploded with sparks showering them. The feelings of our love could be described as safe and content. While it was pleasurable, it did not hold the adventure I so crave. You should have heard the fervor in his voice as he claimed my soul last night. It tore me to pieces while completing me."

"Kathleen, from what I have gathered, Devon has ruined you as not only as Scarlet, but also as Kathleen. Am I correct?"

"Yes."

"You cannot refuse his suit. I will convince Rory of Devon's innocence. But the next time Devon calls, for he will call again, you must allow him a moment of your time. Forgive him. You are angry at him for loving both of you."

"I cannot, nor will I marry him. I realize I have deceived him, but he does not know. I will not marry a man who will betray what our very union would stand for."

"But Kathleen, Devon ruined you. If Rory ever finds out, he will force Holdenburg and you to wed. You must accept him on your own terms."

"Rory will never find out, will he? You promised your secrecy. Also, I will never marry another man. My love for Holdenburg will never diminish."

"Kathleen—"

"Dallis, I understand you want me to find happiness. However, I only want my heartache to disappear."

"Neither your mother, nor Devon's, will allow that. How will you explain your change of heart to them?"

"I won't have to. In time, Devon will show his true colors. He will find interest in somebody else and I will have their support and sympathies."

No matter what excuse Dallis came up with to change Kathleen's mind, Kathleen would find a reason to refute it. So when Kathleen excused herself to help Mama in the garden, Dallis didn't protest. Dallis decided to pay a visit on Devon, to hear his side of the story. If Rory wouldn't confide in her, then she would make Devon tell her the truth.

Chapter Eighteen

Dallis waited for Devon to join her in the Norbrooke's parlor. She left the house, hoping upon her return she could convince Kathleen to talk to Devon. With Rory away at Lord Hartridge's, and Kathleen and Mama working in the garden, it had been easy to sneak away.

Instead of Devon, the Duchess of Norbooke entered with a maid carrying a tea tray. Once the maid had served them, Devon's mother relaxed in a chair.

"Devon is unavailable for visitors today. Can I be of assistance?"

"No, I must speak with Devon."

The duchess arched her brow at Dallis's intimate nature in calling her son by his Christian name. However, the duchess wouldn't intimidate Dallis. Devon had become a worthy friend during their courtship, and Dallis always referred to him by his given name. She wouldn't change her behavior for proper etiquette. Dallis was under the opinion that Devon's mother liked her. The few occasions they visited, the duchess had shown her nothing but kindness. But now she regarded Dallis with a protective nature.

"I understand you have developed a friendship of sorts with my son. I am also aware of the time he spent courting you. Lady Beckwith filled me in on how she persuaded Devon to court you to make Rory jealous and to bring him to heel. She also led me to believe that Rory and you held a faithful marriage. You must be aware how improper your actions are to call on a bachelor as a married lady. Any notions you may have of Devon's affections are for naught. If your visit today was brought to light, and most servants *do* gossip, then your behavior will cause many problems for you, my dear. Not to mention the strain on both our families with your marriage to Rory, and Devon and Kathleen practically engaged. Devon spoke of his wishes and how they are waiting for Rory to give his permission. You understand, it would be best if you were to leave. Any ideas towards Devon must be forgotten. I will hold your visit today a secret and nobody will be the wiser."

Dallis sighed. Her Grace stood correct. Dallis's behavior appeared highly improper and could cause its own scandal. But the duchess was wrong on the reason behind her visit. Dallis wasn't here for herself, but for Kathleen. She hoped to convince Holdenburg to speak the truth of his involvement with Kathleen's father.

"Duchess, you are mistaken on my reason for visiting Devon." Dallis continued to use Devon's name to show she wouldn't be so easily dismissed.

"How so?"

"Kathleen is the reason for my call. I have news Devon would like to hear. They had a minor spat and I want to help him win Kathleen back."

"What has he done now?"

"I cannot divulge that information, Your Grace. Kathleen swore me to secrecy. I can tell you they must admit to their genuine feelings and share complete honesty. Their relationship is a web of deceit."

"Lady Beckwith and I were positive they had moved past their differences. We thought they finally saw the love they had for each other."

"Half-truths have blinded their love."

"I apologize, Dallis. I jumped to conclusions about your visit. Devon has not been himself today. He never came home last night, and when he returned it was before the sun rose. After he changed his clothes, Devon left for a spell and returned shortly thereafter. Since then he has paced the house with a restless energy I do not understand. He won't even speak to me. I am worried over his state of mind."

"They had a falling out and Kathleen has refused to forgive him. I came today to urge him not to give up."

"If you can reach him where I cannot, then I will seek him out. My manners were remiss when you arrived. I told the servants Devon was unavailable and I would speak to you instead."

"I understand."

"Please wait here."

Dallis understood the duchess's confusion, but this outing had lasted longer than she expected. Dallis hoped no one was wise to her disappearance.

Devon arrived. "Lady Dallis, what do I owe this pleasure?"

"Devon, stop with the Lady Dallis nonsense. We need to talk about Kathleen."

"The lady no longer requests my suit and therefore I will not discuss her with anyone."

"Bollocks."

Devon raised his brow at Dallis's vulgarity. Yes, he would make a fine duke one day with his expressions. However, Dallis listened to the pain in his voice when he mentioned Kathleen's name. He held himself too stiffly, and a nervous energy crackled with his movements. Devon didn't know what to do with himself.

She said, "What secret do you hold that you cannot share with Kathleen? If you do not answer my questions, then I will confront Rory when I return home."

"As I told you before, it is not my secret to tell. I do not want to cause Kathleen anymore pain."

Well then, Rory would hold her attention this evening. She was determined to hear the truth. Today would be a lengthy one. Already she felt sleepy from the babe. Dallis rubbed her stomach, the stress from the day wearing on her.

Devon knew upsetting Dallis wasn't good for her or the babe. He needed to reassure her and then see her home. If Rory discovered Dallis had called on him, then all hell would break loose. Rory wouldn't stop until he destroyed Devon. The last time they fought, Rory had taken it easy on him. He wouldn't be so lucky the next time. He wouldn't put up a fight. His guilt spoke volumes. Devon had hurt Kathleen, and for that he would take what he deserved.

"Kathleen witnessed you cheating on her with the actress from the theatre. Is this true?"

"No, as I tried to explain, I am innocent. The actress needed my assistance with her costume. When Scarlet tripped over her gown, my arms came around her so we would not end up on the floor. I tried pulling away from her when Kathleen and Rory appeared in the doorway. I swear I did not touch her. There is no other woman I desire to touch but Kathleen."

"I thought that might be the case. The actress made her intentions very clear of her interest toward you. I noticed you kept your distance and only had eyes for Kathleen. Also, I suspected you did not do what they accused you. After you left this morning, I managed to convince Kathleen what she saw was false. Once she opened her eyes to the accurate picture, she came to the same conclusion. But then she made mention of another incident where you were not faithful. That you took another lady to your bed who was not Kathleen. It was *another* woman by the name of Scarlet you have become enamored with. Is this true?"

Dallis had no need for Devon to answer. The guilt in his eyes spoke the truth.

"Devon, how could you? Kathleen loves you."

"And I love her."

"Then why betray her for a moment of lust?"

"Because it was not a moment of lust. It never has been, nor will ever be. Scarlet is the other half of my soul, the same as Kathleen. I live for Scarlet's attention. Kathleen is the companion I crave. I love both ladies as if they were one."

"Tis impossible," Dallis said even though she knew it to be true.

"Is it?" Devon asked.

"What are you implying?"

"They *are* one and the same."

"You know?"

"Yes, but the question is, how do you know, my lady?"

"Belle."

"Ah, the infamous Belle. I suppose Sidney and Sophia are also aware of Kathleen's secret identity?"

Dallis cringed. "Yes, we tried to assist in our own way for the success of your courtship."

"Is that so? May I ask how?"

"Well, Sidney has kept Rory occupied with a project at Lord Hartridge's. I must say it started out as a fluke, but they came across some interesting findings. Why—"

"Dallis," Devon growled.

"Yes, of course ... Sophia hosted the dinner party last week you escorted Kathleen to. You two were not aware, but she held the dinner in your honor. If you recall, it was only a small gathering of family and friends. And perhaps a member or two of the ton who would gossip what a charming couple you made."

Devon remembered that dinner. Kathleen had gazed upon him with adoration. There was never a more perfect evening in their courtship.

"And your assistance?"

"I worked to convince Kathleen of your magnetic attributes and to open her heart to you. Then when Rory was present, I tried to keep him away. I know how Kathleen values her brother's opinion. I had to convince both of them that your pursuit was pure."

"And Belle's hand in all this?"

"Her job was to make sure no harm came to Kathleen. But the greatest harm of all came to her, did it not? Her heart became broken by her own duplicity. She believes you were not aware of her deception as Scarlet."

"Do you think I would not notice how Kathleen presented herself? That woman only needs to be within a few feet from me and I would sense her very presence."

"Then why not reveal her identity?"

"Because when Belle came to me with the news of Kathleen's interest, I choose to allow Kathleen to amuse herself. I never imagined it would spiral out of control. I had hoped she would see past her plans to ruin Lord Velden and myself. Once we moved past her revenge and I won her hand, fate played a cruel twist on us. Now I have lost her and hold no clue on how to regain her love. Her goal is again to destroy me."

"Why did you make love to her? She believes you betrayed her in the worst way."

"Because she tempted me in a manner I could no more resist than I could not breathe. I only meant to play her game, but, well …"

"Never mind, I get the general idea. How will you fix this? You need to express your utter devotion to her."

"How can I without betraying my knowledge? Kathleen would think I played a game with her emotions. Can you not see that I also suffer? The woman I love does not trust in my love. Kathleen believes I would betray her with another. How can we continue, if trust does not lie between us? Also, Kathleen has arranged a card game on Saturday evening against Lord Velden and myself. I received an invitation to join their game this morning. She plans to ruin us then. However, Lord Velden will ruin her. He will see her attempts at cheating a mile away."

"You must try."

"When I left her this morning. I sensed her watching me from the window. I made a promise I would keep returning day after day until she forgave me. But when she pulled her hand away from the window and closed the curtains, I realized right then it was hopeless. No, it would be best for Kathleen to find somebody else."

"But you ruined her. When Rory discovers this, you will not be safe."

"I am tormented by my actions. I have thought of nothing else."

"We must do something to end this madness."

"Dallis, you have never offered me anything but your gift of friendship. Every day since I met you, your acts of kindness have humbled me. However, you must stop. I have made my decision, and Kathleen has made hers. I need you to respect our wishes. Perhaps, in time, we can continue our friendship, but for now we must put a halt to it."

"I understand. I will respect your decision for now. But you must understand this, I will not relent. I will figure a way for you two to be together. It may not be today, or tomorrow, but it will happen. I will keep your and Kathleen's secrets for now. But secrets always come to light and when they do, there will be nothing either one of you can do but to admit to them. Then you will have to deal with your problems. Until then, I hope you will reconsider your decision."

Devon helped Dallis to her feet and called the carriage. As he helped to settle her in the seat, he smiled. The best thing he ever did was to befriend her. Dallis became feisty over her passionate causes. It warmed his heart that she considered Devon one of them. Life would have been so much easier, and so less painful, if he'd pursued Dallis and married her. But Dallis's heart did not lie with him, nor his with her.

Devon reached inside his pocket and pulled out the two tokens that started this complete mess. Devon stared at them for a moment. Part of his conscience urged him to give the coins over to Dallis. If there was any hope to be reunited with Kathleen and for their secrets to be divulged, these coins held the key. Dallis would demand the answers to them.

Dallis watched the indecision cross Devon's face as he stared at the objects in his hand. He stood with the carriage door open, contemplating something. When Devon's gaze rose, his look beheld a determination Dallis hadn't seen earlier. Then, when Devon displayed his charming smile that sent all the women in the ton a flutter, Dallis realized he'd changed his mind. And it had something to do with the two coins.

Dallis held her hand out, and Devon placed the tokens in her gloved palm. He folded her fingers over them and squeezed her hand.

"Present these to Rory and Kathleen together."

Dallis nodded. With another charming smile, he closed the door and gave instructions to the driver to see her home. Dallis relaxed back, opened her palm, and examined the two coins. While similar in shape and texture, they held unique images. One of a boxing ring, the other a deck of cards. These coins held the answers to the questions Dallis would ask this evening.

Chapter Nineteen

After dinner, Dallis requested that the family to join her in the library for a short spell. She had something she wished to share. None of them ever refused Dallis. She had brought much light to their family in a time of darkness, and for that reason, Kathleen followed everyone and settled in a chair near the fire—although Kathleen wished nothing more than to continue up the stairs to her bedroom where she could be alone with her misery.

After the afternoon spent with Mama in the garden, Kathleen wanted to hear the name Devon Holdenburg no more. Her mother praised his attributes and pleaded with Kathleen to forgive him. When Kathleen could no longer stand listening to his glorious character, Kathleen revealed that Devon cheated on her with another. Her mother denied his actions, pleading his innocence, but when she realized Kathleen spoke the truth, she stopped. She held her arms open for Kathleen. Kathleen ran into her mother's embrace and cried as she hadn't cried since she was a young girl. Her mother settled them on a bench and held her, not saying a word. She didn't reassure her with false promises that would never come true. She only rubbed Kathleen's back and dried her tears. Then Mama led Kathleen into the house and made her favorite blueberry scones. Her mother and Agnes bantered back and forth, drawing laughter from Kathleen. Even when Rory came home and wanted to berate Devon, his mother led him away.

Dallis announced, "I have asked you in here because we must discuss what happened the fateful night of your father's last card game. The secret is damaging those we love. Rory, when I married you, I realized you carried many burdens of your father's past sins. The ultimate sin is still kept quiet by you and your mother. After we got married, you swore you would no longer hold onto your secrets. But you have not been honest with me, even after you promised you would be."

Rory and Mama exchanged glances betraying a secret still lay in the dark. It was time for them to speak. When neither one of them made the effort and remained silent, Dallis knew she would have to present the coins. She'd had hoped her speech would prevail and prevent having Kathleen suffer more heartache.

Kathleen looked back and forth from Dallis, Mama, and Rory. What secret did Dallis imply still stayed hidden? Which sin of her father's did they keep from her? Kathleen knew her father had cheated on her mother and gambled their money away. What else?

"Mama? Rory?"

"It is time we tell her, Rory."

"No, our family has gotten rid of Holdenburg, and he will never step foot in this house again. You may have forgiven Holdenburg, Mother, for what he did, but I never will. Dallis, I forbid you to continue your friendship with him."

"Rory, you will forbid me no such thing," Dallis spoke quietly.

The tension in the air kept everybody from speaking. Still, no one confessed the secret.

"Very well, you leave me with no choice. On my visit with Devon this afternoon—" Dallis began.

Everyone in the parlor spoke at once, asking the same questions. When? And why?

"As I was saying, at the end of my visit, Devon asked me to return to our family two items." Dallis slipped a hand inside a pocket and withdrew the two tokens. The colors stood out as beacons on her palm. From their reactions it would appear everyone understood what the coins represented. Everybody but Dallis.

"How did Holdenburg gain those coins?" asked Mama.

Kathleen stayed silent, watching the color drain from her mother's face. Mama knew the story behind the tokens. If Devon gave them to Dallis, then he …

Her face paled along with her mother's. Devon knew Kathleen was Scarlet all along. When he spoke those passionate words last night, he wasn't declaring them to Scarlet, but to her. Kathleen closed her eyes and remembered the desire in his eyes when he'd stared at her naked. *Oh my.* Devon had never betrayed Kathleen; he worshipped her and her alone. What had she done? Kathleen had thrown Devon's love right back into his face.

Dallis said, "From the expression on everybody's face, you understand what these coins represent. Since we are a family, perhaps one or all of you would like to fill me in on what they stand for?"

Dallis sat down on the couch and waited.

"Mama?" Dallis asked.

"The green token was my late husband's coin to gain access into his favorite gaming hell. It was a place he would frequent on a nightly basis, where he lost all our money and gave away a precious gift that was not his to give away."

"What gift was that, Mama?" Kathleen asked.

Rory said quickly, "Mother, say no more. I will confide in Dallis with the truth of Father's sins. Please do not tell Kathleen."

His mother said, "Rory, you have protected our family from your father's indiscretions long enough. It is time for Kathleen to learn the truth. This farce can no longer continue. It is time to end your hatred toward Devon. He was not at fault."

"Father should never have made that bet. Holdenburg taunted Father with a prize, knowing Father would lose. Can you not see Holdenburg has brought Kathleen nothing but pain? If Kathleen hears the truth, it will be a heartache she will never recover from. She had to learn of Holdenburg's scandalous character. Do not ruin the memory of our father too. Father was Kathleen's hero."

"Yes, but even heroes have flaws. And your father had more than his fair share. He was only human, a human who could not resist a temptation he should have avoided. While your father hid his extra-marital affairs well, I will not have Kathleen believing all gentlemen act in the same manner. She has already placed Devon in the same category of your father, and the boy is nothing like him."

"He is worse," growled Rory.

"He is not. Do you think your best friend would betray your friendship on the mere whim of a bet? If your answer is yes, then you never deserved Devon's friendship."

By then Rory's anger had grown further with his mother's adoration of Devon Holdenburg. The man set out to ruin his sister's reputation, and Rory would make sure Kathleen understood who Devon Holdenburg truly was.

"Yes, I do. Devon led Father into laying a bet on Kathleen's virtue and he took great pleasure in winning the bet."

Kathleen and Dallis gasped at Rory's declaration. Each with a different reason, but both knowing Devon didn't make the bet out of spite.

"Is this true, Mama?" Kathleen asked. She didn't trust Rory to speak anything but hatred toward Devon.

"Not the full truth. Yes, he won the hand on where your virtue was at stake. But he was not the one who *placed* the bet."

"Papa?" Kathleen asked.

"No, Lord Velden."

Kathleen sat confused more than ever. She never even met Lord Velden until this season. Why did he make a bet concerning her virtue when he had never met her?

Her mother explained in a heavy voice, "Lord Velden noticed you with your father one afternoon and he wanted you for himself. Father denied Lord Velden's suit when he offered for you. When your father wouldn't even allow Velden to call on you, this angered the lord. So, he tempted your father after he was well into his cups to a game of cards. As the evening progressed, the bets became more outlandish. Devon urged your father to walk away from the game. But your father was stubborn and tried to win his money back. When your father had nothing left to lose, Lord Velden threw down the gauntlet. If he won the next hand, then your father must consent to a marriage between you two. If Velden lost, then he would walk away and never try for your hand again. Devon watched Lord Velden cheat throughout the evening and realized your father was too drunk to win. So, Devon inserted himself into the game. When they showed their cards, Devon held the winning hand. Not only had Devon won the hand, but all of your father's fortune and *you*. Devon called on me the next day and tried to explain about the game. The guilt the boy has worn on his sleeve every day since then has ate at him. Then, when Rory refused to believe his reason for injecting himself into the game, he has been miserable ever since. He tried to return the money, but I refused. I told Devon the truth would come to light and for him to show patience. When Kathleen allowed Devon to court her, I thought we had put the past behind us. But I feel something transpired last night, destroying our happy ending."

Kathleen sat in shock. What a fool she had been. She'd never imagined her father's demise resulted from him giving his daughter away for nothing but a chance at a win. She looked around the room. Her mother held a look of regret. Rory sat in the same shock as herself. When Kathleen's glance moved onto Dallis, it was to find her friend—nay her sister—smiling with a look of determination.

Could she win Devon back?

When Kathleen looked at Dallis, Dallis nodded yes.

"How?"

"You already know the answer to that question, my dear," Dallis answered.

"How what?" Rory growled.

"Nothing, dear brother."

"Kathleen …"

"Mama?" Kathleen inquired.

"Whatever you must do, I will support your decision."

"I require a new dress."

"What?"

They ignored Rory, discussing what Kathleen would need to wear to win over Devon. Her brother sat confused, staring at the women in his life.

"Rory, I will need your escort to Belle's on Saturday night."

"No," he roared. "Where did you learn of Belle's?"

All the women raised their eyebrows at his ignorance. They laughed.

"I do not enjoy being the subject of my family's humor. You are not stepping foot inside Belle's, nor will you commission a new dress. In my opinion it would be best for you to visit Mama's family in Ireland."

Kathleen rose and went to her brother's side.

"Rory, my dear brother, you have been my rock my entire life and I will always depend on you. But this is something I must do. I must prove to Devon my love. I only hope I am not too late. By not placing my trust in him, I have betrayed him in the worst way possible. I have arranged a game at Belle's between Lord Velden, Devon, and myself. At one time I had hoped to ruin both of them, because of the game that destroyed Father. We were both clueless to the details of the bet. Can you not see we both have misjudged Devon? Does he not deserve more from us? With you escorting me, he will see it as an offer of renewing your friendship. Please Rory, I love him so."

Rory sighed. He could never deny his sister. This was another instance where his father created a mess that he must clear away. Holdenburg had tried to explain the scope of Rory's father's bet and why he had intervened. But Rory's rage wouldn't allow him to see reason. Rory had seen the attention Holdenburg paid towards Kathleen and realized his friend desired more. When he heard Holdenburg wiped out his family's finances and won the virtue of his sister's innocence, Rory only wanted to beat the man senseless—and he did. Holdenburg stood there taking Rory's pounding fists, never once deflecting a blow. Even when Rory knocked him down and wrapped his hand in a death grip with his bones cracking, Holdenburg never fought back.

To Rory, that only proved the devious workings of his friend's mind. That was the day Rory no longer called Holdenburg a friend, but an enemy. His sister's innocence was her own to give to whomever she loved. His father's bet went against every grain Rory believed him to be. While he was alive, his father protected and coddled Kathleen as a precious daughter. Rory questioned what brought his father to those depths of depravity? Maybe only Holdenburg could show insight to an answer.

Then shortly thereafter his father passed away in his mistress's bed. A scandal bringing shame upon their family. Soon invitations stopped, and nobody called. It was only upon the good graces of the Hartridges' that the scandal became swept under the rug. Lord Hartridge's standing with the Crown caused many in the ton to turn a blind eye to Rory's father's affairs. Before long, the invitations returned, and their parlor filled once more. They weren't shunned for very long. The only sad part of the entire ordeal was that his family still suffered for a while. His father left them destitute with not a shilling to their name. With his quick mind, and the brute of his fists he helped them recover. After he married Dallis, they settled into a comfortable lifestyle. They used her dowry to invest in some wise business ventures, and they were now stable.

Looking back, Rory realized he'd blamed the wrong man. Even throughout Rory's anger, Devon still called on his family, offering his friendship. Yes, Kathleen stood correctly. They had both wronged

Holdenburg. Only his mother regarded him with care. When Kathleen spoke of Devon, her eyes reflected the love she felt. The same love he shared with Dallis. Once again, Rory wouldn't deny Kathleen's wishes.

"All right. This goes against every rational argument I might have, but I will help you. Only on the condition that Sheffield and Wildeburg accompany us. You do not comprehend the nature of Lord Velden's character. He is a dangerous chap. He will have his own men spread throughout the gaming hell. Do not think for one second you will be safe."

Kathleen said, "I disagree. You are wrong on Lord Velden's character. He is perfectly harmless. The two times I have been alone with him, he has acted the perfect gentleman. Well, except for that one kiss."

Kathleen flinched when her brother suddenly towered over her in anger.

"What kiss?" he growled.

"At the theater when I became lost. He attempted to kiss me."

"And you allowed him to?"

"He kissed me before I even realized his intent. Then he apologized."

"Is Holdenburg aware of this kiss?"

"No," Kathleen winced.

"When he finds out, he will be furious."

"There is no need for him to find out."

"Kathleen, this only proves how naïve you are. Lord Velden will make Holdenburg aware of the nature of your kiss. Please tell me you slapped the reprobate for taking what you did not offer?"

"No, I ... might have told him his kiss was pleasurable."

"Why the hell would you do that?" Rory bellowed.

Dallis said, "Rory, calm down. Shouting at Kathleen won't solve the problem we have to contain."

"My sister has no clue what Pandora's Box she has opened. And she imagines a simple card game will solve all her problems. She does not understand the full extent of this dilemma. Mother, would you care to explain to Kathleen and Dallis the implication of Lord Velden's affections?"

His mother said, "Yes, I see I must be completely honest. I had hoped to avoid this subject. But if we are confessing our secrets, then I must tell them the reason for Lord Velden's attentiveness."

Kathleen told them, "You think he is the evil villain in this story, but both times he only came to my assistance. At the Camville Ball I became lost in the garden maze. Lord Velden helped me to find my way out. The next time, I became separated at the theater when somebody stepped on the back of my dress, and Lord Velden stopped my fall and saw me to safety before I fell flat on my face. Then he walked me to the actress's room. Like I said, both times a perfect gentleman."

"Kathleen, a perfect gentleman is not the term most would speak of this particular fellow. For you to do so, only proves we have been lax in watching over your welfare. You cannot even call Lord Velden a scoundrel, for he is the devil in sheep's clothing."

"You are mistaken, Mama."

"No, Kathleen, I am not. Lord Velden has wanted possession of you for many years. Not to marry you, but to *own* you. He offered marriage because that was one way to get his hands on you. But once he married you, you would be under his devious control. Your father refused his offers and kept him away. However, Lord Velden devised a plan to have you. In time, he acquired all of your father's markers from his losses spread around town. When your father had no more to give, Velden waved an offer in your father's face. Your father, the fool that he was, thought he could beat Lord

Velden at his own game. He tried every trick in the book to beat the man. Only your father lost. Then on the last hand Velden offered your father all his markers and the chance for you to keep your virtue. If not, then he would own all. Well, we know how that card game ended. Devon has since kept Lord Velden at bay all these years, keeping him away from our family. Devon holds more power than Lord Velden ever will. However, now you have tempted Velden with your innocent kisses, he will never relent."

"I never imagined what I had unlocked by visiting Belle's."

"So that is the reason Devon had those tokens. Why the hell did you go there?" Rory demanded.

Kathleen said, "I had hoped to help to ease our family's financial burden, but my ultimate goal was to see those two men ruined. Along the way, I fell in love with Devon."

"Why the hell did Belle not inform me of your hi-jinks?"

"Perhaps because she informed me instead," Dallis said. She was the one who winced now.

All eyes swung to Dallis. Mama smiled with approval and Rory glared his disapproval of Dallis having anything to do with Belle's establishment. With Belle herself, he had no problem—hell, Belle needed more friends. And if his wife was one of them, he wouldn't object. Belle had been more than a friend to him during his time of need.

Kathleen's look was one of confusion.

"You knew the entire time and never once divulged my secret?"

"It was not my secret to tell."

"I will agree to any plan you come up with, Rory, as long as I can prove to Devon of my love and our family's forgiveness. Call upon your friends while Mama and Dallis help me to design a dress."

Rory agreed and sent word to Sheffield and Wildeburg to come over and to bring their scheming wives. Sophia and Sidney were two of the most devious women he knew.

Before Kathleen offered her suggestions, she flipped the two coins in her hand. She had already devised a plan to prove her love and forgiveness to Devon. Kathleen smiled, hoping she'd receive the reaction she imagined.

Chapter Twenty

With a sense of doom, Devon entered Belle's gaming hell. The evening didn't hold for a promising ending, but one that must be met. He heard no word from the Beckwith residence. Devon had at least hoped Dallis would tell him the reaction from the two tokens. But nothing. When his mother tried to reach out, Lady Beckwith replied with apologies, explaining how their family was dealing with a personal crisis and she would respond soon.

Belle had greeted him when he arrived like she always did. She never uttered a word of anything unusual in play. Belle didn't mention Kathleen either, now that he thought about it. He was sure Belle would have least inquired as to the status of their relationship.

This evening would be his last spent with Kathleen. By now she knew that he had known of her identity the entire time. That when he seduced Scarlet, he'd made love to Kathleen. Devon's words of utter devotion were for no other woman but Kathleen alone. Holdenburg would play the game of cards and protect her from Lord Velden. After Kathleen won her victory, Devon would turn his back on her forever. With no word from her this week, it only meant one thing. Kathleen didn't forgive him, and she never would. Devon could no longer endure remaining in London and watching Kathleen from afar. He'd acted the part for too many years already. Devon would retire to his home outside of London, the same home he'd purchased for them to live their lives together. He would reside there and become a country gentleman—a lonely country gentleman, because no lady but Kathleen would do. Devon would find comfort from the memories they shared on their one fateful afternoon—memories that would have to last him a lifetime.

When Devon walked into the noisy room, the tables were full as usual and the drinks stayed filled. A few of Belle's girls were draped across the gentlemen's laps, offering words of encouragement among other things. Belle had sequestered a table near the back of the hell for their game. She posted Ned and a few other guards near the wall. As Devon walked to the table, he noticed Lord Velden already held reign with his lackeys near him. Velden commanded the chair resting against the wall so he could see the viewpoint of the entire room. The only chair remaining at the table sat with its back to the room. It would appear Devon held the disadvantage this evening. He could sit on either of the sides, but only one chair sat in the middle. It must belong to Kathleen, because a drink rested next to a reticule. She'd already arrived. Why did Belle keep Kathleen's arrival a secret? Where was Kathleen now? Lord Velden held a smirk of satisfaction of his time spent alone with Kathleen. Devon tightened his fist, wanting to take a page out of Rory's playbook and slug the bastard. But Holdenburg needed to show his calm façade if he were to get through this card game. No, he wouldn't give Lord Velden the satisfaction.

Devon turned, searching for any sign of Kathleen. Perhaps he should find her and convince Kathleen to stop this madness and explain what Lord Velden really wanted. Something he should have explained all along, instead of caving into her need for a sense of adventure. Now Devon was too late. Or was he? Devon started back for the door, not stopping even when Lord Velden called out his name.

Devon stopped mid-step when Kathleen appeared in the doorway. She left him speechless. There standing before him was the vision he had dreamed about. A fantasy she'd never fulfilled until now. A gown of the darkest sapphire adorned her body, draping her curves in silk. The gown rested off her shoulders, leaving her creamy shoulders bare and rested low. Kathleen's breasts pressed high, begging to be released with one deep breath. She'd styled her hair loose, the long dark tresses brought over one shoulder and held with a bejeweled clip. Kathleen wore the dress for him. Devon raised his gaze to find what he wished for, but his wish was instantly replaced with fear. Kathleen gazed at him with love—however, her face lay exposed.

She didn't wear a mask.

Devon advanced on Kathleen with a purpose she hadn't expected. She wanted to see his gaze filled with passion, perhaps the love he spoke of, since she wore the dress to spark his desire. Kathleen only saw fear and anger in Devon's eyes. She took a step back then stopped. No, Devon wouldn't intimidate her. She had a plan, and he wouldn't stop her from achieving it. Instead, Kathleen lifted her chin and sauntered toward Devon. When they met, she looked him in the eye. He didn't back down and tried to grab her arm to steer Kathleen out of the room.

The appearance of her brother halted Devon's intent when Rory stepped in front of Kathleen.

"Holdenburg."

"Get the hell out my way, Beckwith. Are you both mad?"

"It would appear so," Rory answered.

Kathleen tugged on Rory's arm to move him out of the way. She heard the tension in Devon's voice and he showed an intensity she'd never seen before. It would appear she had much to learn of Devon Holdenburg. Kathleen always took him for granted. Devon had always been a calm figure in her life. She had misjudged him. After talking with Dallis, Kathleen realized she owed Devon so much more than an apology and her love. Kathleen owed him devotion and passion from her soul, because that's what Devon had given Kathleen all these years without her knowledge. The time had come for them to get this card game over, so she could repair the hurt she caused.

"You are late for our card game, Lord Holdenburg. Shall we?"

Kathleen didn't wait for his reply and walked to the table, Rory following closely behind. Devon looked around, wondering if he was in a play. Was he the only sane person in this gaming hell? Why did everyone act that her appearance was the norm? Kathleen sauntered around the gaming hell as if she was born here. Yes, she could play a game of cards better than any gentleman here. But the scandal of an innocent debutante playing with the degenerate gentleman of the ton inside a brothel would ruin her from ever entering a ballroom again.

Devon paused, taking a closer look at the gentlemen sitting at the tables. They were not Belle's usual crowd. No, these men were friends of Sheffield, Wildeburg, and Rory's. Even a few of his friends from his school days filled the tables. Scattered among them were gentlemen Lord Velden had made an enemy. When he looked back at Kathleen, he saw her wink and tip her head as in 'Shall we' before she slid into a seat. Why that devious minx ... what game did she play now?

Devon continued to the table, pulling out a chair and sitting down. He never once changed his expression. Whatever Kathleen planned, he needed to pretend anger at her deceit.

Devon baited Kathleen. "It would appear, Lady Kathleen, you have deceived us. What happened to the delectable Scarlet? I quite enjoyed the pleasure of *her* company."

"Yes, well, you know how I love the theater, and how my greatest wish is to be an actress. I could not resist pretending to be somebody I wasn't. Also, it helped me to gain entry into Belle's."

Lord Velden laughed. "What a hoot. You are telling me you held no clue the two women were the same? Especially since you courted Lady Kathleen? I realized the moment I set eyes on Scarlet. And you were practically her betrothed. But no longer, from what the gossip whispers."

"No, I did not." Devon spoke through gritted teeth while glaring at Kathleen, making his displeasure known by all.

"Even when you tasted her charms? I must admit I became quite angry when I heard you had beaten me yet again. But then I am sure you are not aware of the kiss Lady Kathleen and I shared. The sweetest encounter I have ever had."

Devon leapt across the table and swiped the smug grin off Lord Velden's face, sending him sprawling backwards and hitting his head on the wall. Devon didn't stop there. Before Velden could recover, Devon pounded into him again until someone pinned Devon's arms behind his back and dragged him away.

"Devon, stop," Kathleen cried.

Devon shook himself free. He ran a hand threw his hair, shooting a glare at the woman he thought he loved.

"How could you?"

Kathleen winced. Rory warned her that Lord Velden would gloat to Devon that he kissed her. She foolishly thought he wouldn't. The pain lacing Devon's voice caused her to reach out to touch him, only for him to pull away in disgust. Now she understood how Devon felt when Kathleen thought he had betrayed her. Helpless.

Lord Velden wiped the blood from his face and rose laughing from the floor. The bastard took pleasure in watching them suffer. Devon wanted to hit him again.

Rory said, "Easy friend, he will get his due."

Devon turned and arched his brow. "Friend?" His voice dripped with sarcasm.

"Yes, friend. Trust in Kathleen," Rory whispered, before he helped Kathleen back into her seat.

Kathleen spread her hands inviting each gentleman to take their places. When they sat down, she bestowed a smile on them before waving the dealer over to start the game.

Kathleen grew nervous about continuing the charade, aware of Devon's anger that he tried to bring under control. He clenched and unclenched his fists upon the table top. Making everyone aware of his unleashed fury. Kathleen needed to control the situation, and she also wanted to ease Devon's plight. First things first, they needed to rid themselves of Lord Velden before she confessed her love to Devon. Again, Kathleen wanted to reach out and squeeze Devon's fingers to prove she was his, but she didn't want to play her hand too soon.

"Lord Velden, please forgive Lord Holdenburg for his outburst." Instead of touching Devon's hand she reached for Lord Velden's instead. She caressed the tips of his fingers before moving up his arm. She attempted to seduce him with a smile.

Kathleen wanted to cringe at her seductive attempts on Lord Velden. She must convince him of her interest to draw him into her web. Kathleen realized it worked when, with a predatory gleam, Velden smiled at Devon.

She said, "You know we shared our kiss in private and you promised not to tell a soul. For shame, my lord."

"Yes, well, a man must brag when he tastes something so sweet. It is his glory to best another. I have wished to taste those sweet lips upon mine for a long time. I am most proud to have done so."

Kathleen blushed under his warm speech. She encouraged more compliments with each stroke of his arm. Kathleen wanted Velden so enamored with her, he wouldn't realize when she deceived him to win. Because from what she had learned from Belle and Rory, the only way to best Lord Velden was to cheat first, and best. Velden might be a skilled player, but in turn he resorted to cheating when he couldn't win. That was how he had beaten her Papa all those years ago.

"Shall we, gentleman? Both of you have promised me a game of cards."

Trust Kathleen. Those were the words Beckwith whispered. However, Devon was hard-pressed to put his faith in a woman who stroked a hand up and down his enemy's arm. To Devon it appeared Kathleen was trying to seduce Lord Velden. Devon looked more closely at Kathleen. He took in the grace of her body. He almost believed her performance, except Kathleen gave away a hint of her deception. One would know this slight detail only if they had known Kathleen her entire life. Kathleen's other hand rested in her lap with fingers crossed. He wanted to laugh at the innocent gesture, but it would give away whatever she had planned for Lord Velden's demise.

Whenever Kathleen pretended, cheated, or lied, she would always cross her fingers. Devon looked up to find Rory's eyes on him. Devon gave Rory a slight nod, indicating he was onto their game. Yes, trust Kathleen.

"Excuse me, I need a drink."

Devon shoved his chair back and stalked over to the bar. With instructions to the barkeep, he ordered a bottle of vodka. After receiving his bottle he returned to the table, taking a long swig. He observed the two of them with their heads bent together whispering of God knows what while he drank a third of the bottle.

"Are we going to play cards, or would you two prefer to get a bedroom upstairs?" Devon slurred.

Kathleen frowned at Devon, sliding away from Lord Velden. His garbled speech suggested he might not be dependable. Had Kathleen pushed her flirtation with Lord Velden too far?

"Perhaps you should quit drinking, Devon?"

"Madam, you may no longer request I put a stop to any of my actions. When you slammed the door in my face a few days ago, you gave up your rights. Now I shall only ask one more time, shall we?" Devon nodded at the dealer waiting to deal the cards.

Kathleen nodded. Devon's crushing words left her wondering if he meant what he said. She only cared for his welfare and didn't like when he drank himself into a stupor.

Soon the game began. Each of them winning a few hands. Kathleen won without any deception and felt confident that she could end this farce soon. However, the next few were not in her favor or Holdenburg's. By now Devon had drunk the entire bottle of vodka. A drink so harsh that it left many men unable to stand, let alone play cards. Devon continued to play, just not with his usual skill. He also slumped in his chair. Not once through the entire game did he speak. Even when Lord Velden and Kathleen's heavy flirtation led to Velden fondling Kathleen, Devon never uttered a sound. Did Devon not care?

Soon the pot filled. When it came time for Devon to raise the bet he pulled out of the game, slurring his excuse of a bad hand. He folded the cards and leaned back in his chair, smirking at the two of them. Devon's expression held many mysteries to which Kathleen didn't hold a clue. The game now stood between Lord Velden and Kathleen. Kathleen pushed all her chips into the middle of the table and turned a flirtatious smile onto Lord Velden. He returned her smile with one of victory, making her skin crawl. Velden accepted her bet and raised it.

"It would appear, my lady, you are out of chips. However, I will be generous with my offer. I will extend the same deal to you which I made to your father. Your father accepted, and you seem more than willing too. If I hold the winning hand, you will be mine. I can no longer make the offer of marriage since Lord Holdenburg has already sampled your charms. No, I require an innocent lady for a bride. You shall do nicely as a mistress. Do not fear, my lady, I shall take better care of you than I would my bride."

"I will take your offer with pleasure, my lord," Kathleen purred. "And if I should win?"

"Whatever you desire, my dear," he purred back, pulling Kathleen's chair closer, his hand resting under her breast.

Several men were instantly ready to pull Lord Velden away. Rory pressed down on Devon's shoulder, pushing him back down in his chair. Kathleen swatted Lord Velden's hand away.

"Now, now, my lord. You must wait until you win before you play," Kathleen laughed.

Kathleen didn't pull away from Lord Velden, as much as she wanted to. No, she relaxed in his hold taking pleasure that she would soon shock him with a winning hand.

"If I beat you, then you shall stop all attempts in your pursuit of me. You will accept I will never be yours and turn your attention onto a soul more deserving of your attention. You will never dishonor my name."

Lord Velden laughed at her petty stakes. Did this bitch think she would win? Even if she did, he would take great pleasure on bringing her to task. He had wasted enough years chasing her skirts, and he meant to have her before this evening was through. Nobody would stop him, not the man sitting across from him, and sure as hell not her brother who stood waiting to slug him. No, she would spread her thighs for him tonight. After he pounded his cock into her thoroughly many times, he would spread enough gossip to ruin their family forever. He'd had enough of the Beckwith and Holdenburg families.

"I accept your terms, my lady. Now allow me to show my cards first."

Lord Velden laid down four kings.

His smile held the smugness of victory. "Shall you dismiss your brother or shall I?"

Devon whistled. "Why, Velden, you played one hell of a hand. It looks like you have finally won the sweet lass. That is unless she holds a better hand. Show us your cards, my lady." He was no longer slurring, his voice loud for the entire room to hear.

"Oh, my. That is an excellent hand, my lord. However, I shall be the victor this evening."

Kathleen flipped her cards over one by one. She started with the smallest face value, displaying her straight flush. All hearts. The queen of hearts seemed to wink at them.

Lord Velden flipped his chair over as he rose, "You filthy cheat. You do not differ from your father. Hell, I should have known when we played you would stoop to the same level as him."

Velden advanced on Kathleen, grabbing her arm and dragging her from the chair. His grip tightened causing Kathleen to scream in agony. When Rory tried to intervene, Lord Velden's men stepped in front of them. He then twisted one arm behind her back, continuing her pain.

"You bitch, did you think I would allow you to win? No, you are mine. Nothing and not a single soul will stop me from taking you. Holdenburg stepped in last time and took what was mine, but not again."

Kathleen whimpered, her arm twisted at an odd angle where she was unable to fight back. She tried to turn around and break out of his hold like Rory taught her, but Velden's grip remained clenched too tight.

Devon flew out of his chair, advancing on them. All rational thought left his mind when he saw Kathleen being abused by the hands of this snake. He roared his anger and tried to break through the defenses, but there were too many of Lord Velden's men. Rory, Devon, and Belle's men kept pounding, but they wouldn't drop fast enough. Lord Velden dragged Kathleen towards the exit. He had to be stopped before they left, or getting Kathleen back would be difficult. Lord Velden kept his home like a fortress.

Every gentleman at the tables rose and blocked the doorway. They took up spots around the room, blocking Velden from escaping with Kathleen. Each man advanced on Lord Velden.

"Unhand her, Velden," Sheffield ordered.

"Never."

"Your reign of destruction has ended. The men in this room have come to an agreement. If you leave London peacefully, they will destroy your markers. You are never to contact Lady Kathleen or make any attempts on her again. I will only say this once. If you do not comply, then I will hold no responsibility for their actions. Unhand Lady Kathleen now."

Lord Velden thought he could outsmart all the men present. He thought his men would protect him. But he was wrong. Not only did they refuse to protect him, they pointedly moved well back. They realized the power in the room and wouldn't risk their lives for him. However, Velden wasn't finished. He pulled a knife out and held it forward, inching his way backward.

Devon froze for only a second when Lord Velden flashed his knife. His fear for Kathleen kept Devon from attempting to pull her out of Velden's grasp. The man was mad. Devon glanced over at Rory, sending him a silent message. Rory nodded. Each man went to opposite sides and worked their way in. Sheffield noticed what they attempted and kept ordering Velden to give Kathleen up. Once Velden became distracted enough, Rory and Devon pounced. Rory pulled Kathleen out of Velden's arms and Devon kicked the knife out of his hand. Then Devon threw the bastard a punch, knocking him on his ass—and Devon was far from satisfied with just that. He'd spent years dealing with this piece of scum. He pounded into Velden for every second he held Kathleen in pain. Sheffield and Wildeburg tried dragging him away, but Devon threw them off.

It was only when Devon felt the soft touch of Kathleen's hand that he halted. Kathleen pulled him away. Her soft tone tried to calm him. When Devon saw how much Kathleen was in pain, he stopped. She stood back, staring at him while holding her arm. Waiting. All he could do was stare. With one last kick at Lord Velden, Devon stalked away past Kathleen to the bar and pulled out a bottle of whiskey from behind the counter and returned to the card table.

Kathleen watched Devon grab another bottle. He kept ignoring her. She thought he would welcome her back with open arms. However, Kathleen had bruised Devon's ego with her lack of trust. She turned back to Lord Velden. He lay beaten and bruised on the floor. Rory touched her shoulder in concern. Kathleen shook her head and looked back at Devon.

"Go talk to him," Rory urged. "We will take care of Velden."

Rory, Sheffield, Wildeburg, and the rest of the men carried Velden from the room. Sheffield's power in the ton would keep Velden from bothering Kathleen and her family ever again.

Belle entered the room and stood in the doorway. She arched her eyebrow and nodded toward Devon. Kathleen returned her nod. Before the evening had begun, Kathleen made a request to Belle. Belle agreed, promising Kathleen and Devon privacy after they destroyed Velden.

Belle smiled her encouragement and closed the doors. Kathleen listened to the click of the lock. Kathleen stood alone with Devon. But did Devon want to be alone with her?

Kathleen turned toward Devon to see him slung low in his chair with his back to her. His clothes were disheveled, and he kept tipping the bottle to his mouth, taking long slugs. Between this bottle and the bottle of vodka he drank while they played cards, Devon would be incoherent before long. Kathleen took a deep breath and walked behind him.

Kathleen laid a hand on his shoulder. His muscles tensed from her touch, but he didn't turn around. She noticed his hands were bloody and bruised. When she tried to soothe him, Devon jerked away and took another swallow from the bottle.

Devon's emotions ran riot. He couldn't handle Kathleen's touch yet. There were too many unanswered questions. The whole evening confused him. Devon took another drink. He hoped the alcohol would help him to understand, but the more he drank, the more confused he became.

Kathleen ached for any kind of sign from Devon. When he continued to ignore her and refuse her affections, she felt she wouldn't be able to reach him. Kathleen walked around the table to the dealer chair. She shuffled the deck, then dealt them each one card.

"High card wins. The winner gets to choose anything they want. Whatever decision they make for the future, the loser must accept. Do you accept those conditions, Lord Holdenburg?"

Kathleen had left the decision to Devon. Did he want those terms? Devon wanted so much more, but feared Kathleen no longer wished the same. *Trust Kathleen*. Rory's words kept chanting over and over in Devon's head. He'd never stopped trusting in Kathleen, she was the one who gave up on him. Even if he won and staked what he desired, Devon couldn't live his life always under suspicion. He understood Kathleen's hesitation. The knowledge of her father's double life now led Kathleen not to trust any man. But Devon wasn't the late Lord Beckwith. Devon was his own man and Kathleen needed to realize that.

Devon shoved all his coins to join Kathleen's winnings from Lord Velden.

"I will raise you, Lord Holdenburg." Kathleen smiled.

Devon watched Kathleen slide two tokens across the table at him. The same tokens he had returned to Dallis earlier this week, which created this drama. Devon stared into Kathleen's eyes and saw how nervous she was. Devon realized her fear, if he should refuse her.

"I have nothing to raise with."

"I suppose you can offer a request, if you win."

"And if I lose?"

"I will allow you to choose that too."

Devon now understood where he stood with Kathleen.

"If I win, then you will share my bed every night until I deem I no longer desire you."

"And if you lose?" Kathleen whispered, unsure. His bet left too many questions of his intentions.

"If I lose, then I will be at your disposal for whatever you desire."

"And if I desire only you and you alone?"

"Well, I must lose for that to be possible."

"I *can* arrange it."

"Mmm," he murmured.

Kathleen flipped her card over. The same queen of hearts twinkled at them.

When the card flipped over, he already knew what would stare at him from across the table. He would have to teach Kathleen how to cheat better. She was horrible at it. He saw her make the switch when she shuffled. It was the same as when Kathleen played against Velden. Devon watched the change and knew Velden saw it too.

Devon took another drink. His hands still shook from reaction after seeing Kathleen being tormented at that man's hands. Kathleen had played a dangerous game tonight.

Kathleen saw the indecision on Devon's face. He still hadn't flipped over his card. He continued to drink from that damn bottle.

"Well, my dear, I fear your luck for the night has ended."

Devon flipped over his card and would have laughed at Kathleen's expression, but he continued to keep his gambling face firmly held. He had his own tricks up his sleeve. And Devon would trick Kathleen into believing he only wanted a brief moment of her time alone. Then, once he had her to himself, he would never let her go.

The king of hearts laid next to her queen. Devon had won. How? Kathleen dealt him the jack of hearts.

Devon rose from his seat. "Shall we?" He indicated for them to leave.

Kathleen rose with dignity. Never let it be said she didn't lose with grace. Devon offered no words of humor and displayed no affection. Kathleen must face that Devon only meant to use her until he was ready to move onto another woman. Kathleen had made her bet and lost. She tried to open the door but whimpered when the pain in her arm prevented her.

Devon ached to comfort Kathleen. But he needed her alone and away from anybody who would stand in his way. Devon reached to open the door and guided Kathleen along the hallway. Once they reached the exit, Rory and Belle waited for them.

Rory reached his hand out. Devon looked at him and then shook Rory's hand. The evening had brought about many changes, and they still had much to resolve. After he'd finished with Kathleen, then Devon would have a lengthy discussion with Rory. One they should have shared many years ago. Back then perhaps, if Devon had forced the issue, none of this would have happened.

When Rory reached for his sister, Devon pulled Kathleen to his side, careful of her arm. Devon's hold spoke of his possession.

"You will see her home?" Rory relented.

"No, she will reside with me until I decide differently. Only when I am done with her will I release Kathleen back into your care."

"The hell you say. Kathleen?" Rory growled.

"I am fine, Rory. Lord Holdenburg has won my company until he tires of me. I will not relent on my wager."

"Let go of her, Holdenburg. I recant my offer of friendship. You are no better than Lord Velden."

"I am sorry you think so lowly of me, my *friend*." Devon emphasized the term. "However, many years ago, I stood back and did not call on the terms of the bet I won from your father, fair and square. I even tried to relinquish the bet, but your mother refused. Now, only a few minutes ago, your sister agreed to the terms of a new bet. She lost. This time I have collected, unlike the last marker I won from your family. Now, if you do not mind, I have had a long evening and I want to enjoy my bed." With this he brought Kathleen against his body, allowing his hand to rest beneath her breasts. He displayed his full intent and threw it in Rory's face.

Belle watched the power play between the two men and knew if she didn't deflect this situation there would be more fighting. One bloodied member of the ton was enough for one night. Belle wanted neither of these men hurt. You only had to look at Lady Kathleen to see she didn't protest Holdenburg's embrace. If anything, she took great pleasure at being held in his arms. Devon's display of possessiveness declared his intentions. She saw the emotions that Holdenburg tried to contain and that he kept a tight rein on his temper. If she didn't persuade Rory to allow Devon to leave with Kathleen, then she didn't know what would come to light.

Belle pulled Rory away. "Rory, you know the rules of my house. I am sure if you allow Lord Holdenburg to take your sister away, he will return her in the morning, where you shall see that all is well. Am I correct in my assumption, Lord Holdenburg?"

Devon didn't answer. He didn't have to explain his actions to a damn soul any longer. Their relationship had been controlled by too many parties. Both of their mothers, Rory, Lord Velden and countless others. Well, no longer. Devon didn't wait for Rory's agreement.

He swept Kathleen out of Belle's and into his carriage.

Chapter Twenty-One

Kathleen laid in bed waiting for Devon. When they had arrived at his house in the country, she wasn't prepared for the comforts he provided. She expected him to whisk her to his bedroom where he would make mad passionate love. Damn Dallis and her romance novels. But that was exactly what she had expected. Hoped for. Dreamed of. None of that transpired. After showing Kathleen to a bedroom, decorated in softer shades of blue, a maid arrived to see to her care. Devon had ordered a warm bath. The maid assisted Kathleen and took care not to harm her arm.

After the bath, the maid apologized for having no nightwear for her and brought in a man's nightshirt. She explained it was one of Lord Holdenburg's. Kathleen thanked her and explained it would do. When the maid gathered her clothing and left the room, Kathleen rubbed her hands up and down the sleeves, taking comfort from Devon sending the nightshirt. She imagined the sleeves as his arms holding her.

Another knock sounded on the door, and once more Kathleen was disappointed. The housekeeper carried a tray with tea, and the local doctor followed. The doctor examined her arm, assuring Kathleen it wasn't broken. It would show bruising and be tender for a few days. He instructed Kathleen not to lift anything heavy and to prop her arm while sitting or sleeping. He gave her a sedative and insisted she should rest.

Kathleen lay down and fought the drug that the housekeeper made sure was taken with the tea. She was resigned to the fact that Devon wouldn't be joining her this evening. Why did he bring her to his home if he didn't plan on collecting his bet? What was his agenda?

Kathleen yawned and snuggled deeper into the bed, wishing Devon had joined her. She wanted to rest her head on his shoulder and find safety in his embrace. Kathleen's anger and need for revenge had worn her out. Kathleen only wanted to love Devon.

Her eyes drifted closed. The last thought before she drifted to sleep was of the card he threw down. The cheater.

~~~~~~

Devon lifted the covers away from Kathleen and stared down at the beauty before him. When the doctor told him Kathleen would recover and there were no lasting damage from Lord Velden's abuse, Devon breathed a sigh of relief.

Kathleen moaned and rolled over on her back, his nightshirt sliding up her thighs. Oh, the sweet temptation before him. How easy it would be to slide between Kathleen's thighs and take her. Devon knew she wouldn't protest, —she hadn't complained of anything since he won the hand of cards. Kathleen appeared more than eager to accompany him home. Devon knew he was an ass at Belle's, but he wanted them to be alone. And for that to happen, he had to act as the indifferent cad that he wasn't.

It was the only way to get past Rory and Belle.

When Devon next took Kathleen, it wouldn't be while she was under the influence of medicine. After the sedative wore off, they had much to discuss. Then and only then would he never surrender his hold on her. For

Devon would never tire of his desire for Kathleen. She was his for an eternity.

He lifted her from the bed, pulling her closer.

"Devon," she murmured in her sleep.

"Shh, love. Go back to sleep."

"Mmm." Kathleen snuggled closer.

Devon carried her next door to his bedroom. This was where he had wanted Kathleen since he brought her here, but he didn't want the servants to gossip. He laid her on the bed and joined her. Devon pulled the blanket over them and held Kathleen while she slept, not once taking his eyes off her. Kathleen's hand nestled on his chest, where he slid his hand over to hold hers. Devon kissed the top of her head as Kathleen sighed into him.

"I love you, Kathleen," Devon whispered.

Kathleen, in a fog, thought Devon carried her into his bed. She wanted to respond but was too sleepy. Kathleen took comfort from his embrace. When he whispered those simple words, Kathleen knew their relationship would survive. *I love you too, Devon*, she meant to say, returning his sincerity, but fell back asleep instead.

~~~~~~

Kathleen awoke in a warm and comfortable bed. Not wanting to rise yet, she kept her eyes closed. Kathleen snuggled into the warmth surrounding her body. She squirmed to get closer, not quite wanting to awaken.

"Lay still, minx. Can you not see, I still sleep?"

Kathleen's eyes flew open at Devon's sleepy drawl. She lay facing him as he tried to sleep. Memories from the night before came flooding back. The drama from Lord Velden and her final bet with Devon. The last thing she remembered before falling asleep was waiting for Devon to come to her bed. But he never did. He must have though, because she no longer remained in the other bedroom. Kathleen lay wrapped in Devon's arms. He must have carried her in during the night. Did this mean what she thought it meant? Or was Kathleen only here for his pleasure until he tired of her? Did Devon mean what he said to Rory? Whatever his reasons may be, Kathleen wouldn't object. While Kathleen wanted Devon forever, she would at least stay with him for as long as Devon wanted.

Kathleen reached out to brush a hand across his whiskered cheeks, enjoying the rough texture. How would those feel against her skin? Would they tickle or increase the pleasure of Devon kissing her?

Devon savored her exploration and didn't move as she caressed his cheek. Even when her hand slid lower, he never moved a muscle. However, when Kathleen's lips followed the trail of her fingers, Devon couldn't stop the moan he released. Nothing had ever felt so sweet. Each brush of her lips sent his body aflame. Kathleen kept moving lower, her hand brushing across his hardened cock. Still, Devon didn't stir, afraid this was all only a dream.

Devon hadn't moved a muscle. Kathleen knew Devon was awake. She held proof in her hand. Long, hard proof. He held his body in anticipation. Kathleen wouldn't disappoint his pleasure, stroking her tongue along his hardened length. While Kathleen loved Devon with her mouth, she felt the slight twitching of his hand in her hair. Kathleen smiled, sucking her lips around the tip of his cock, her tongue licking off his juices.

Kathleen followed her return along Devon's body by sliding her body over him. She pressed a soft kiss on the edge of his lips.

"Dev, are you going to sleep the day away?"

Devon opened one eyelid at her teasing. Devon saw the woman he loved staring at him with her own love shining from her eyes. A teasing smile lit her face, but he also noticed a woman's desire—someone who he needed to please. Far be it for Devon to refuse pleasuring a woman.

Devon flipped Kathleen over, drawing her closer. His hand reached between her thighs; Kathleen's wetness coated his fingers. Devon didn't wait, but slid inside Kathleen, her body arching into his.

Once Devon settled deep inside Kathleen, he stared down at her. Her eyes, clouding over with desire, stared back. "No, love, sleep is not what I had in mind for the day." He slid in deeper, drawing her leg higher around his hip.

Kathleen moaned as Devon filled her soul. With every stroke of his body, her body followed. With every caress, her body arched into his. With every kiss he drew from her lips, she savored. As Devon consumed Kathleen with his passion, her body clung to him, begging him to never stop.

The higher their passion grew, the tighter they clung to each other. Never wanting to let go for fear they would lose each other again. Just before Devon sent them over the edge he paused, gazing at Kathleen with an emotion for which there were few words. Only three simple ones, that Kathleen felt just as deeply.

"I love you," Devon whispered again.

Kathleen clung to Devon as he swept her away, too choked to respond. Telling Devon that she loved him would never be enough. The emotions she held were more than that.

"Kathleen?"

"Mmm?"

"You are not falling asleep, now that you have woken me."

"Mmm."

Devon chuckled, drawing Kathleen onto his chest. He would allow her a light doze before they had their discussion. They had much to clear the air on. After their lovemaking, Devon felt secure that all would be well with them. Eventually he must return her home. Only long enough until they wed. But not too soon. Devon meant what he said, that what he had planned today was more than sleep. Devon wanted to enjoy Kathleen all day. Then maybe he would return her home this evening. If not, Devon would have to deal with one very angry brother.

~~~~~~~

The next time Kathleen awoke, it was to the aroma of fresh blueberries. She was ravenous. When she opened her eyes, it was to find a tray full of blueberry scones next to her pillows. When she reached for her favorite treat, she heard Devon laugh.

"I thought those would wake you, lord knows I could not."

Kathleen blushed, drawing the blanket around her tighter. Even through all her brazen acts, Devon could still make her blush. Especially when she rolled over and saw him lying naked, propped up against the pillows. As Kathleen bit into the scone, her eyes traveled the length of Devon. She would never tire of gazing at him. When Kathleen noticed how hard Devon was, the laughter in his eyes changed at her perusal.

"You can eat later." He took the scone from her hand, throwing it on the tray as he gathered her to him.

Devon's lips devoured Kathleen as a man obsessed. Each kiss he drew from her lasted longer than the last. She drew her breaths from him. Kathleen wrapped her arms around him, keeping him held to her.

Devon meant for them to talk while Kathleen ate. But one glance of her eyes on him, as innocent as they may have been, was more than Devon could handle. His need was stronger than ever. He wanted to start every day with Kathleen like this.

Devon's hands stroked down Kathleen's body. Her breasts grew heavy in his hands, molding them to his touch. He played with her nipples until they became tight buds, each of them begging for his attention. When Devon's hand traveled lower, Kathleen opened her thighs at his silent command. His fingers sunk into her wetness and he groaned his desperation. Devon slid his finger inside, and Kathleen responded by pressing into him, her hips arching, wanting more.

Devon wouldn't refuse Kathleen. He would ease the ache she needed relieved. With resistance, he pulled away from her lips. Kathleen reached out to draw him back, but Devon had another idea on how he would pleasure her.

When Devon pulled away, Kathleen felt the loss immensely. She needed him.

"Devon," Kathleen pleaded.

Devon gave her a wicked look right before he dripped honey across her breasts, coating her nipples. Kathleen gasped when she realized his intent. When he continued to drip the warm honey between her thighs, Kathleen was no longer shocked but curious. She would soon discover the sweet pleasure of his lips licking the honey off.

Devon stroked his tongue around her breasts, savoring the sweet treat. When his mouth sucked the nectar from her nipples, his senses exploded. Mixed with Kathleen's sweetness, it was a flood of pleasure. Devon drew her nipples between his lips, sucking every drop of honey away. After he ate his treat away, he followed the path of his desire.

Kathleen lost all sense as his lips savored the honey from her body. She yearned to explore the unfamiliar sensations Devon stroked to life. When Devon slipped between her thighs, Kathleen opened herself to him. His fingers trailed the honey around as his lips followed. Kathleen closed her eyes and arched her wetness toward his mouth. She needed him to kiss her. Kathleen's body ached for Devon's mouth. When he spread the warm honey across her desire, Kathleen whimpered her need.

"Devon," Kathleen pleaded again.

Oh, sweet mercy. She was divine. Kathleen lay spread before him, opened for his pleasure, moaning his name with her need. Devon watched the honey slowly slide along her wetness, clinging to her clit. When her hand slid through his hair, urging his head to her, Devon obliged. With pleasure.

Devon stroked his tongue along the length of Kathleen for his first taste of her honey sweetness. It wasn't enough. Devon craved more. His mouth took possession of her wetness. Devon devoured every drop of honey from Kathleen. His tongue slid over and over the sweet coating on her clit, sucking the sweetness between his lips.

Kathleen grasped his head tighter as he devoured her, responding as he drove her body to a place only he could with the stroking of his tongue. Kathleen came undone under his hunger.

The moment Kathleen released, Devon savored the sweetness in his mouth. While her body floated on the pleasure from his tongue, he slid his hardened length deep inside her. Kathleen throbbed and clung to Devon's cock as he took her body higher, wanting her to come undone with him.

"I love you," Kathleen moaned over and over. Kathleen clung to him, giving Devon her heart, body, and soul.

~~~~~~~

In the bath, Devon ran the damp cloth over Kathleen's body, washing the honey away. When he noticed the bruises covering her arms, he called himself a bastard for forgetting about her injury. In Devon's uncontrollable desire, he'd neglected to give Kathleen the care she needed.

"I am a brute." Devon dropped the cloth and caressed Kathleen's arm.

Kathleen had forgotten about her injury once she had woken in his arms. She rolled over in the water, resting her forehead against his, staring Devon in the eyes.

"No, you are not."

"Yes, I am. I should have been taking care of you, not ravishing you like a madman possessed with making you his."

"Well, I quite enjoyed having a mad man ravish me. Do you think he will make another attempt?" Kathleen asked, pressing her chest against his, her nipples raking over him.

"Kathleen," Devon warned.

"Yes, love?" Kathleen asked, rising to straddle him.

Devon tipped his head back against the bathtub in sweet agony. Kathleen's exquisite body was a temptation he couldn't refuse. Nor did he want to.

Kathleen smiled, watching Devon trying to resist her. She knew he was mad at himself for neglecting her injury, but he didn't need to be. Her arm no longer hurt. Kathleen shifted her hips and slid Devon inside her. He gripped the tub tighter and Kathleen smiled more. When she slid up and back down quickly, Devon lifted his head and pierced Kathleen with a look searing her soul. As she rode him faster, he groaned her name louder. Soon Devon clung to Kathleen, pressing himself to her, pounding up into her, taking over. Devon lost control, sending them beyond all they knew but could only wonder about.

Devon lay back in the water, pulling Kathleen with him. He would never have enough of her. They needed to dress, or else he would keep her captive for the rest of the day in their bedroom. Not his—theirs. It had always been theirs ever since he bought the estate.

"Love?"

"Mmm, yes?"

"I fear that we must talk."

"I know."

Devon heard the fear in her voice and wanted to reassure her. But first they must get dressed. With her naked, it wouldn't take long for their discussion to become distracted.

When Devon lay there and didn't make an attempt to talk, Kathleen grew confused. Should she start with an apology or wait for him? He kept calling her love, and his lovemaking was playful, but that could mean anything? Right?

"Love?" he repeated.

"Yes?"

"We need to get dressed."

"Oh."

Devon rose from the tub and dried himself off, wrapping the towel around his waist. He helped Kathleen out and wiped the water from her body. When he saw the uncertainty in her eyes, he reassured her.

"If I am to stay sane, then clothes must cover your body. If after our conversation you find happiness in the outcome, I will be more than willing to let you take advantage of me again."

Kathleen's face lit up, her doubt fleeing at his wicked, teasing smile. Devon grabbed her hand and guided her to a door through which Kathleen saw the room she fell asleep in the night before.

"I will send a maid to help you dress, and then she will lead you to the gardens where we will talk. Is this all right with you, my lady?"

"Yes, my lord." Kathleen stood on her tiptoes and placed a kiss on his lips before closing the door.

Chapter Twenty-Two

Kathleen found Devon in the garden, sitting at a table with two chairs. On the table rested a pot of tea and a plate of blueberry scones and honey. He rose when Kathleen arrived and helped her into a seat.

"Since I ruined your breakfast, I thought you would enjoy your blueberry scones while we talked."

"I quite enjoyed the distraction, but I am famished." Kathleen winked at him.

"Then by all means, my dear, allow me to be your humble servant."

Kathleen laughed at Devon's teasing and knew in her heart all would be well with them. She gazed at him adoringly as he poured a cup of tea and served the scones.

After Kathleen finished eating, Devon explained his past actions. He kept touching his fingers to hers. Devon communicated his feelings with soft caresses.

"Kathleen …"

"I am sorry, Devon, for ever doubting you," Kathleen interrupted him.

"Shh, love. I need to explain myself. Because of my deceit, I made it possible for you to not trust me. I am sorry. I should have told you the truth from the very beginning."

"None of it matters anymore."

"No, it doesn't. But nonetheless, I want you to know."

Kathleen nodded, taking his hand.

"It all started many years ago. One day you were this pest, always following Rory and I around. Then next, I was a besotted fool wanting to follow *you* around. I did not realize when it happened. I only knew you'd captured my heart, and I became smitten."

"But you never followed me anywhere, you were always so cruel."

"That was because I did not understand my newfound devotion to you. Plus, I sort of followed you. Do you remember those private acting lessons my father arranged for you?"

"Yes."

"I convinced my parents to allow me to escort you to the theater and guard against any untoward actions from the actors. It was my chance to be alone with you."

"But you never were alone with me. You always deserted me to fool around with any girl who would flash a smile your way."

"That is what I led you to believe. I tried to get any reaction from you, to see if you felt the same way. I never fooled around with them, I sat in a seat in the back and enjoyed your delight at acting. When you would never respond to my flirtations, I kept trying harder."

"And you said I held no skills in the acting department. But I fooled you. Your disappearances with different actresses crushed my soul. Then when you returned, your hair and clothes were mussed. You sat across from me with a smile full of satisfaction. And every time, I would hurt that you never took notice of me."

"But I did. I only told you of your inability to act, because I grew tired of escorting you and suffering the indifference you regarded me with."

"Why did you not share how you felt?"

"You were too young, Kathleen. So I waited until you came of age."

"And in the meantime?"

"The meantime is my past. I hope you are my future."

Kathleen pouted. His past relationships had fueled the gossip of the ton for years. Every single woman who played a part in his past, she hated them, envied them, hurt for them when Devon discarded them. Because the hurt they endured was the same as hers. Devon Holdenburg was an addiction from which you could never recover.

She said, "Carry on with your explanation."

Ahh, he would have to soothe her battered emotions before he was through. Devon only hoped Kathleen would forgive him.

"Then during your first season, I approached your father with my request. My confidence was high and my ego just as high. I never imagined your father would reject my suit. But he did. Only he didn't reject me, he swore it would never happen. I did not understand why. Our families were longtime friends. Hell, Rory, and I were best mates. Why would he refuse me?"

"Why did he?"

"Because of all the trouble Rory and I had gotten into over the years. He thought I would only bring you trouble and heartache. He saw how I went through woman after woman, and he did not believe I could be faithful to you. I tried to show him how I had changed and would never hurt you, but he refused. Even your mother tried on my behalf, but your father refused her too."

"They never told me. Why did you not try again?"

"Because shortly thereafter your father passed away and the circumstances surrounding your father's death did not paint me in a very good light."

"Mama explained, Devon. I now understand what happened that fateful night."

"I had to, Kathleen, I refused to allow your father to hand you over to that bastard. He had no right. All for a win. Lord Velden's obsession with you was known by all. Your father refused him too. Because of the very reason he refused Lord Velden, he allowed Velden to swindle him."

Kathleen rose and slid onto Devon's lap, wrapping her arms around him. Devon still held onto anger toward her father that he needed to let go.

Devon took comfort in Kathleen's affections, but needed to finish his story.

"Once I won the hand, I made it clear to Lord Velden to never go near you or I would destroy him. I had no words for your father. A man I once admired now only held my disgust. A few days later, your father passed away. The guilt from that game ate me alive, so I paid a visit to your mother. The devastation your mother was subjected to because of your father angered me. I told her of the card game and tried to give back your father's money. But she refused. When I tried giving back the marker for your hand, she shocked me with her reaction."

Kathleen said, "My mother has told me you won the hand with honesty, and one day you would win my hand with the same true integrity."

"Yes, your mother has always been my strongest supporter."

"Then why did you allow her to convince you to court Dallis?"

"Because she called on a favor. She decided it was time to move forward in life. That her family had suffered enough from your father's disgrace. I was to court Dallis to make Rory jealous enough to act, and to make *you* jealous enough to admit your feelings toward me. She also hoped along the way that Rory and I would repair our friendship. Once he had discovered his father's bet, Rory never forgave me. He would never listen to my explanations."

"He will now. We both have opened our eyes to see how we have misjudged you. I am sorry, Devon, for sending you away."

"You know your reason for sending me away was because of my actions to love you?"

"Yes, but I believed you did not know who I was. That you had fallen for Scarlet."

"Ah love, Belle told me of your plans before I introduced myself to Scarlet. But she wouldn't have had to say a word, I would have known you anywhere, no matter how you disguised yourself."

Devon kissed Kathleen on the shoulder, his lips leaving a trail of fire. She arched her neck to give him better access. When Devon pulled away, Kathleen pouted.

"I am not finished."

"You are a tease, Lord Holdenburg."

He smiled. "I gave Dallis those coins, hoping for any sign of your understanding or forgiveness. I never imagined last night's outcome."

"When Dallis presented our family the coins, she made us open up to be honest with one another. Mama explained why we needed to forgive you. Then we came up with a plan to bring Lord Velden to his knees. Rory called in his favors with the help of Sheffield and Wildeburg. I could not tell you I had forgiven you, because I needed your hurt and anger toward me to fool Lord Velden. Then when you started drinking heavily and your anger grew out of control, I realized that not confiding in you about our plan was a mistake."

"Kathleen, love. I was not drinking."

"But you finished an entire bottle of vodka. I watched you."

"No, the barkeep switched the bottle out with water. When Rory whispered to trust you, I started to watch you closely. You were acting. It was then I decided to play along. I wanted to tear that man apart when you flirted with him."

"My skin still crawls from his touch. But it worked. Velden is out of our lives, isn't he?"

"Yes, love, he will no longer be a bother."

"Can you ever forgive me for not trusting in you?"

"If you will forgive me for not being honest with you?"

Kathleen placed her hands on his cheeks and kissed him gently on the lips, then put her head on Devon's shoulder. They still had much to discuss, but Kathleen knew in her heart they would have a lifetime to share their thoughts and feelings. For now, Kathleen only wanted to enjoy the comfort of Devon's love.

Devon held Kathleen close, her kiss giving him the answer to all his doubts.

"I need to return you home before Rory sends out a search party."

Kathleen stiffened. He was sending her home? But she had thought …

"Please, Devon, do not send me away. Not yet."

He tipped her chin up.

"I'm not *sending you away*. I only spoke those words last night, because I wanted you to myself and I did not want to fight Rory. And, I admit, a part of me wanted to see your reaction. Your trust humbled me. Believe me, I have no intention of ever sending you away."

"But you said you were returning me home."

"Only long enough for our mothers to plan a wedding."

"A wedding?"

"Yes, love."

"Whose?"

"Ours."

"Mmm, you never mentioned a marriage. I do not recall that being part of the bet."

"Perhaps you did not hear the terms of the bet clearly?"

"No, I heard them very clearly. You declared I was yours until you tired of me, then and only then would release me."

"Well, my lady, I will never release you. You are mine for eternity."

"Eternity is quite a long time, my lord."

"Kathleen," Devon growled. "You cannot renege from the terms."

"Double or nothing? If I win, you agree to renegotiate the terms."

"And if you lose?"

"I will not lose, my lord."

"You cannot cheat this time."

"As if I ever would."

Devon waved a footman over and requested a deck of cards. Once he held the cards, he shifted Kathleen on his lap and pulled the deck out. This time he would control the cards.

"We will make this simple. We each will draw from the middle of the stack. High card wins."

"Agreed."

"Ladies first."

Kathleen pulled out her card and showed it to Devon.

Devon closed his eyes at her card. An ace of hearts. Her smile was full of gloating. He pulled out his card at threw it on the table face-down.

Kathleen said, "As I told you, I never lose."

"Mmm. What are your terms?"

"That you call off the terms of your bet."

"Never."

"But I won."

"Did you? You have not seen my card."

Kathleen reached for his card and flipped it over. An ace of hearts. How?

"It would appear we have a draw, my lady."

"You cheated."

Kathleen grabbed the deck out of his hands and turned them over. Every single card was an ace of hearts until she reached the end of the deck. Where a king and queen of hearts rested.

He said, "I will cheat every day for a chance to awaken with you in my arms. I will cheat for any chance to have your sweet lips touch mine every day. I will cheat to have your love as your husband."

"You will never have to cheat, for I will awaken you every day with a kiss full of love as your wife."

Kathleen kissed Devon with her promise.

Epilogue

Finally, their guests had departed. After Devon dismissed the servants for the evening, he went in search of his wife. Today was their six-month anniversary and Devon wanted to give Kathleen a surprise.

Devon found Kathleen in their bedroom. She was wearing nothing but a robe. He smiled, pleased that she shared the same idea. Kathleen gazed out the window to the garden below their balcony. The moon lit the frozen ground. He came behind her, wrapping his arms around and pulling her in close.

"Devon, what is that resting between our benches?" She pointed to where they would sit and enjoy the outdoors.

"I had a swing built for next summer. I thought Morgan would enjoy it."

Devon used Rory and Dallis's daughter as an excuse. It would be for their own child. But he didn't want to ruin Kathleen's news. Devon waited patiently for Kathleen to tell him.

Kathleen turned around. "You are a sweetheart, Devon Holdenburg."

She pulled his head down for a kiss. Kathleen held such love for this gentleman. While he had portrayed himself as a scoundrel to the ton, he was anything but that. The love Kathleen held for Devon grew with each day.

One kiss was all it took for Devon to want Kathleen. He undid the ribbon on her robe and spread it apart. She stopped him.

"Not now, love. I want to play one hand of cards before we retire."

"Ah, Kathleen, later. I only want to love you now. I promise we will play cards all day tomorrow. While we entertained our families this evening, I waited patiently to have you to myself. I wanted to share our anniversary alone."

"You must learn patience, my love."

Kathleen pulled herself out of his arms. "We can even play in bed." She wiggled her eyebrows at him.

Devon sighed. He could never refuse Kathleen.

Kathleen crawled into bed and pulled a deck of cards out of the drawer. Devon frowned when she unwrapped a new box. Kathleen had a pack made special for this evening. They were not your usual cards; each was blue or pink with a matching color of an ace on the front of the card.

Devon slid in next to Kathleen and saw the odd color of cards. Then he realized this was how she would share her news. Barely containing her excitement, Kathleen's hands shook. She was adorable.

"What does high card win this time?" he asked.

Kathleen didn't answer but held out the deck to him, and he pulled out a card. Kathleen didn't pull one out. Devon lifted the card to see the king and queen of hearts holding a baby ace in their hands.

"A lifetime of happiness." Devon answered, pulling Kathleen into his arms, the cards falling all around them. "I adore you, my sweet wife." He unwrapped her and rested his hand on her stomach.

Kathleen gazed into Devon's soulful eyes, lost to the magic of his love.

"I love you, Devon. Are you thrilled?"

"More than you can imagine. We can begin to fill our garden with running urchins."

"Our children will not be urchins. Hustlers perhaps, but never urchins."

"Ah, I will love every rascal and minx as much I love you, my darling Kathleen."

Devon took Kathleen's lips into a passionate kiss displaying to her all the love he felt. They celebrated their anniversary long into the night and early morning with each of them secure in the trust they had built and continued to build. With every game they played together neither one of them came out the loser. They both were winners at heart.

~~~

I cannot end this series without giving Belle her own happily ever after. If there was ever a lady who deserves this more, it is her. She has watched all of her friends find true love, now it is time for Belle to find hers.

Read Belle's story in The Forgiven Scoundrel

~~~

Visit my website www.lauraabarnes.com to join my mailing list.

~~~

"Thank you for reading The Scoundrel's Wager. Gaining exposure as an independent author relies mostly on word-of-mouth, so if you have the time and inclination, please consider leaving a short review wherever you can."

Desire other books to read by Laura A. Barnes

Enjoy these other historical romances:

Fate of the Worthingtons Series
The Tempting Minx
The Seductive Temptress
The Fiery Vixen
The Siren's Gentleman

Matchmaking Madness Series:
How the Lady Charmed the Marquess
How the Earl Fell for His Countess
How the Rake Tempted the Lady
How the Scot Stole the Bride
How the Lady Seduced the Viscount
How the Lord Married His Lady

Tricking the Scoundrels Series:
Whom Shall I Kiss... An Earl, A Marquess, or A Duke?
Whom Shall I Marry... An Earl or A Duke?
I Shall Love the Earl
The Scoundrel's Wager
The Forgiven Scoundrel

~~~~~

Author Laura A. Barnes

International selling author Laura A. Barnes fell in love with writing in the second grade. After her first creative writing assignment, she knew what she wanted to become. Many years went by with Laura filling her head full of story ideas and some funny fish songs she wrote while fishing with her family. Thirty-seven years later, she made her dreams a reality. With her debut novel *Rescued By the Captain*, she has set out on the path she always dreamed about.

When not writing, Laura can be found devouring her favorite romance books. Laura is married to her own Prince Charming (who for some reason or another thinks the heroes in her books are about him) and they have three wonderful children and two sweet grandbabies. Besides her love of reading and writing, Laura loves to travel. With her passport stamped in England, Scotland, and Ireland; she hopes to add more countries to her list soon.

While Laura isn't very good on the social media front, she loves to hear from her readers. You can find her on the following platforms:

You can visit her at **www.lauraabarnes.com** to join her mailing list.

Website: **http://www.lauraabarnes.com**

Amazon: **https://amazon.com/author/lauraabarnes**

Goodreads: **https://www.goodreads.com/author/show/16332844.Laura_A_Barnes**

Facebook: **https://www.facebook.com/AuthorLauraA.Barnes/**

Instagram: **https://www.instagram.com/labarnesauthor/**

Twitter: **https://twitter.com/labarnesauthor**

TikTok: **https://www.tiktok.com/@labarnesauthor**

BookBub: **https://www.bookbub.com/profile/laura-a-barnes**

Printed in Great Britain
by Amazon